Goldwin Smith

Life of Cowper

Goldwin Smith

Life of Cowper

ISBN/EAN: 9783337191368

Printed in Europe, USA, Canada, Australia, Japan

Cover: Foto ©Raphael Reischuk / pixelio.de

More available books at **www.hansebooks.com**

COWPER.

CHAPTER I.

EARLY LIFE.

COWPER is the most important English poet of the period between Pope and the illustrious group headed by Wordsworth, Byron,
and Shelley, which arose out of the intellectual ferment of the
European Revolution. As a reformer of poetry, who called it
back from conventionality to nature, and at the same time as the
teacher of a new school of sentiment which acted as a solvent
upon the existing moral and social system, he may perhaps himself be numbered among the precursors of the Revolution,
though he was certainly the mildest of them all. As a senti-
mentalist he presents a faint analogy to Rousseau, whom in natural
temperament he somewhat resembled. He was also the great poet of
the religious revival which marked the latter part of the eighteenth
century in England, and which was called Evangelicism within the
establishment, and Methodism without. In this way he is associated
with Wesley and Whitefield, as well as with the philanthropists of
the movement, such as Wilberforce, Thornton, and Clarkson. As
a poet he touches, on different sides of his character, Goldsmith,
Crabbe, and Burns. With Goldsmith and Crabbe he shares the
honour of improving English taste in the sense of truthfulness and
simplicity. To Burns he felt his affinity, across a gulf of social cir-
cumstance, and in spite of a dialect not yet made fashionable by
Scott. Besides his poetry, he holds a high, perhaps the highest
place, among English letter-writers ; and the collection of his letters
appended to Southey's biography forms, with the biographical por-
tions of his poetry, the materials for a sketch of his life. Southey's
biography itself is very helpful, though too prolix and too much
filled out with dissertations for common readers. Had its author
only done for Cowper what he did for Nelson ! *

William Cowper came of the Whig nobility of the robe. His
great-uncle, after whom he was named, was the Whig Lord Chan-

---

* Our acknowledgments are also due to Mr. Benham, the writer of the Memoir prefixed to the Globe Edition of Cowper.

cellor of Anne and George I. His grandfather was that Spencer Cowper, judge of the Common Pleas, for love of whom the pretty Quakeress drowned herself. and who, by the rancour of party, was indicted for her murder. His father, the Rev. John Cowper, D.D., was chaplain to George II. His mother was a Donne, of the race of the poet, and descended by several lines from Henry III. A Whig and a gentleman he was by birth, a Whig and a gentleman he remained to the end. He was born on the 15th November (old style), 1731, in his father's rectory of Berkhampstead. From nature he received, with a large measure of the gifts of genius, a still larger measure of its painful sensibilities. In his portrait by Romney the brow bespeaks intellect, the features feeling and refinement, the eye madness. The stronger parts of character, the combative and propelling forces, he evidently lacked from the beginning. For the battle of life he was totally unfit. His judgment in its healthy state was, even on practical questions, sound enough, as his letters abundantly prove; but his sensibility not only rendered him incapable of wrestling with a rough world, but kept him always on the verge of madness, and frequently plunged him into it. To the malady which threw him out of active life we owe not the meanest of English poets.

At the age of thirty-two, writing of himself, he says, " I am of a very singular temper, and very unlike all the men that I have ever conversed with. Certainly I am not an absolute fool, but I have more weakness than the greatest of all the fools I can recollect at present. In short, if I was as fit for the next world as I am unfit for this—and God forbid I should speak it in vanity—I would not change conditions with any saint in Christendom." Folly produces nothing good, and if Cowper had been an absolute fool, he would not have written good poetry. But he does not exaggerate his own weakness, and that he should have become a power among men is a remarkable triumph of the influences which have given birth to Christian civilization.

The world into which the child came was one very adverse to him, and at the same time very much in need of him. It was a world from which the spirit of poetry seemed to have fled. There could be no stronger proof of this than the occupation of the throne of Spenser, Shakspeare. and Milton by the arch-versifier Pope. The Revolution of 1688 was glorious, but unlike the Puritan Revolution which it followed, and in the political sphere partly ratified, it was profoundly prosaic. Spiritual religion, the source of Puritan grandeur and of the poetry of Milton, was almost extinct; there was not much more of it among the Nonconformists. who had now become to a great extent mere Whigs, with a decided Unitarian tendency. The Church was little better than a political force, cultivated and manipulated by political leaders for their own purposes. The Bishops were either politicians or theological polemics collecting trophies of victory over free-thinkers as titles to higher preferment. The inferior clergy, as a body, were far nearer in character to Trulliber than to Dr. Primrose ; coarse, sordid, neglectful of their duties, shamelessly addicted to sinecurism and pluralities, fanatics in their Toryism and in attachment to their corporate privileges, cold, rationalistic and almost heathen in their preachings, if they preached at all. The society of the day is mirrored in the pictures of Hogarth, in the works of Fielding and Smollett; hard and heartless polish was the best of it; and not a little of it was *Marriage à la Mode*. Chesterfield, with his soulless culture, his court graces, and his fashionable immoralities, was about the highest type of an English gentleman; but the Wilkeses, Potters, and Sandwiches, whose mania for vice culminated in the Hell-fire Club, were more numerous than the Chesterfields. Among the country squires, for one Allworthy or Sir Roger de Coverley there were many Westerns. Among the common people religion was almost extinct, and assuredly no new morality or sentiment, such as Positivists now promise, had taken its place. Sometimes the rustic thought for himself, and scepticism took formal possession of his mind; but, as we see from one of Cowper's letters, it was a coarse scepticism which desired to be buried with its hounds. Ignorance and brutality reigned in the cottage. Drunkenness reigned in palace and cottage alike. Gambling, cock-fighting, and bull-fighting were the amusements of the people. Political life, which, if it had been pure and vigorous, might have made up for the absence of spiritual influences, was corrupt from the top of the scale to the bottom: its effect on national character is pourtrayed in Hogarth's *Election*. That property had its duties as well as its rights, nobody had yet ventured to say or think. The duty of a gentleman towards his own class was to pay his debts of honour and to fight a duel whenever he was challenged by one of his own order; towards the lower class his duty was none. Though the forms of government were elective, and Cowper gives us a description of the candidate at election-time obsequiously soliciting votes, society was intensely aristocratic, and each rank was divided from that below it by a sharp line which precluded brotherhood or sympathy. Says the Duchess of Buckingham to Lady Huntingdon, who had asked her to come and hear Whitefield, " I thank your ladyship for the information concerning the Methodist preachers; their doctrines are most repulsive, and strongly tinctured with disrespect towards their superiors, in perpetually endeavouring to level all ranks and do away with all distinctions. It is monstrous to be told you have a heart as sinful as the common wretches that crawl on the earth. This is highly offensive and insulting; and I cannot but wonder that your ladyship should relish any sentiments so much at variance with high rank and good breeding. I shall be most happy to come and hear your favourite preacher." Her Grace's sentiments towards the common wretches that crawl on the earth were shared, we may be sure, by her Grace's waiting-maid. Of humanity there was as little as there was of religion. It was the age of the criminal law which hanged men for petty thefts, of life-long imprisonment for debt, of the stocks and the pillory, of a Temple Bar garnished with the heads of traitors, of the unreformed prison system, of the press-gang, of unrestrained tyranny and savagery at public schools. That the slave-trade was iniquitous hardly any one suspected ; even men who deemed themselves religious took part in it without scruple. But a change was at hand, and a still mightier change was in prospect. At the time of Cowper's birth, John Wesley was twenty-eight, and Whitefield was seventeen. With them the revival of religion was at hand. Johnson, the moral reformer, was twenty-two. Howard was born, and in less than a generation Wilberforce was to come.

When Cowper was six years old his mother died ; and seldom has a child, even such a child, lost more, even in a mother. Fifty years after her death he still thinks of her, he says, with love and tenderness every day. Late in his life his cousin, Mrs. Anne Bodham, recalled herself to his remembrance by sending him his mother's picture. "Every creature," he writes, "that has any affinity to my mother is dear to me, and you, the daughter of her brother, are but one remove distant from her ; I love you therefore, and love you much, both for her sake and for your own. The world could not have furnished you with a present so acceptable to me as the picture which you have so kindly sent me. I received it the night before last, and received it with a trepidation of nerves and spirits somewhat akin to what I should have felt had its dear original presented herself to my embraces. I kissed it, and hung it where it is the last object which I see at night, and the first on which I open my eyes in the morning. She died when I completed my sixth year ; yet I remember her well, and am an ocular witness of the great fidelity of the copy. I remember, too, a multitude of the maternal tendernesses which I received from her, and which have endeared her memory to me beyond expression. There is in me, I believe, more of the Donne than of the Cowper, and though I love all of both names, and have a thousand reasons to love those of my own name, yet I feel the bond of nature draw me vehemently to your side." As Cowper never married, there was nothing to take the place in his heart which had been left vacant by his mother.

"My mother! when I learn'd that thou wast dead,
Say, wast thou conscious of the tears I shed?
Hover'd thy spirit o'er thy sorrowing son,
Wretch even then, life's journey just begun?
Perhaps thou gav'st me, though unfelt, a kiss;
Perhaps a tear, if souls can weep in bliss—
Ah, that maternal smile!—it answers—Yes.
I heard the bell toll'd on thy burial day,
I saw the hearse that bore thee slow away,
And, turning from my nursery window, drew
A long, long sigh, and wept a last adieu!
But was it such ?—It was.—Where thou art gone
Adieus and farewells are a sound unknown.
May I but meet thee on that peaceful shore,
The parting word shall pass my lips no more!

> Thy maidens, grieved themselves at my concern,
> Oft gave me promise of thy quick return.
> What ardently I wish'd, I long believed,
> And disappointed still, was still deceived ;
> By expectation every day beguiled,
> Dupe of to-morrow even from a child.
> Thus many a sad to-morrow came and went,
> Till, all my stock of infant sorrows spent,
> I learn'd at last submission to my lot,
> But, though I less deplored thee, ne'er forgot."

In the years that followed no doubt he remembered her too well. At six years of age this little mass of timid and quivering sensibility was, in accordance with the cruel custom of the time, sent to a large boarding-school. The change from home to a boarding-school is bad enough now ; it was much worse in those days.

" I had hardships," says Cowper, " of various kinds to conflict with, which I felt more sensibly in proportion to the tenderness with which I had been treated at home. But my chief affliction consisted in my being singled out from all the other boys by a lad of about fifteen years of age as a proper object upon whom he might let loose the cruelty of his temper. I choose to conceal a particular recital of the many acts of barbarity with which he made it his business continually to persecute me. It will be sufficient to say that his savage treatment of me impressed such a dread of his figure upon my mind, that I well remember being afraid to lift my eyes upon him higher than to his knees, and that I knew him better by his shoe-buckles than by any other part of his dress. May the Lord pardon him, and may we meet in glory !" Cowper charges himself, it may be in the exaggerated style of a self-accusing saint, with having become at school an adept in the art of lying. Southey says this must be a mistake, since at English public schools boys do not learn to lie. But the mistake is on Southey's part ; bullying, such as this child endured, while it makes the strong boys tyrants, makes the weak boys cowards, and teaches them to defend themselves by deceit, the fist of the weak. The recollection of this boarding-school mainly it was that at a later day inspired the plea for a home education in *Tirocinium.*

> " Then why resign into a stranger's hand
> A task as much within your own command,
> That God and nature, and your interest too,
> Seem with one voice to delegate to you ?
> Why hire a lodging in a house unknown
> For one whose tenderest thoughts all hover round your own ?
> This second weaning, needless as it is,
> How does it lacerate both your heart and his !
> The indented stick that loses day by day
> Notch after notch, till all are smooth'd away,
> Bears witness long ere his dismission come,
> With what intense desire he wants his home.
> But though the joys he hopes beneath your roof
> Bid fair enough to answer in the proof,

Harmless, and safe, and natural as they are,
A disappointment waits him even there:
Arrived, he feels an unexpected change,
He blushes, hangs his head, is shy and strange.
No longer takes, as once, with fearless ease,
His favourite stand between his father's knees,
But seeks the corner of some distant seat,
And eyes the door, and watches a retreat,
And, least familiar where he should be most,
Feels all his happiest privileges lost.
Alas, poor boy!—the natural effect
Of love by absence chill'd into respect."

From the boarding-school, the boy, his eyes being liable to in-
flammation, was sent to live with an oculist, in whose house he
spent two years, enjoying at all events a respite from the sufferings
and the evils of the boarding-school. He was then sent to Westminster School, at that time in its glory. That Westminster in
those days must have been a scene not merely of hardship, but of
cruel suffering and degradation to the younger and weaker boys,
has been proved by the researches of the Public Schools Commis-
sion. There was an established system and a regular vocabulary
of bullying. Yet Cowper seems not to have been so unhappy there
as at the private school; he speaks of himself as having excelled
at cricket and football; and excellence in cricket and football at a
public school generally carries with it, besides health and enjoyment, not merely immunity from bullying, but high social consider-
tion. With all Cowper's delicacy and sensitiveness, he must have
had a certain fund of physical strength, or he could hardly have
borne the literary labour of his later years, especially as he was
subject to the medical treatment of a worse than empirical era. At
one time he says, while he was at Westminster, his spirits were so
buoyant that he fancied he should never die, till a skull thrown
out before him by a grave-digger as he was passing through St.
Margaret's churchyard in the night recalled him to a sense of his
mortality.

The instruction at a public school in those days was exclusively
classical. Cowper was under Vincent Bourne, his portrait of whom
is in some respects a picture not only of its immediate subject, but
of the school-master of the last century. " I love the memory of
Vinny Bourne. I think him a better Latin poet than Tibullus, Pro-
pertius, Ausonius, or any of the writers in his way, except Ovid,
and not at all inferior to him. I love him too with a love of par-
tiality, because he was usher of the fifth form at Westminster when
I passed through it. He was so good-natured and so indolent that
I lost more than I got by him, for he made me as idle as himself.
He was such a sloven, as if he had trusted to his genius as a cloak
for everything that could disgust you in his person; and indeed in
his writings he has almost made amends for all. . . . . I remember
seeing the Duke of Richmond set fire to his greasy locks, and box
his ears to put it out again." Cowper learned, if not to write Latin

verses as well as Vinny Bourne himself, to write them very well, as his Latin versions of some of his own short poems bear witness. Not only so, but he evidently became a good classical scholar, as classical scholarship was in those days, and acquired the literary form of which the classics are the best school. Out of school hours he studied independently, as clever boys under the unexact-ing rule of the old public schools often did, and read through the whole of the *Iliad* and *Odyssey* with a friend. He also, probably, picked up at Westminster much of the little knowledge of the world which he ever possessed. Among his school-fellows was Warren Hastings, in whose guilt as proconsul he afterwards, for the sake of Auld Lang Syne, refused to believe, and Impey, whose character has had the ill-fortune to be required as the shade in Macaulay's fancy picture of Hastings.

On leaving Westminster, Cowper, at eighteen, went to live with Mr. Chapman, an attorney, to whom he was articled, being destined for the Law. He chose that profession, he says, not of his own accord, but to gratify an indulgent father, who may have been led into the error by a recollection of the legal honours of the family, as well as by the " silver pence " which his promising son had won by his Latin verses at Westminster School. The youth duly slept at the attorney's house in Ely Place. His days were spent in "gig-gling and making giggle " with his cousins, Theodora and Har-riet, the daughters of Ashley Cowper, in the neighbouring South-ampton Row. Ashley Cowper was a very little man, in a white hat lined with yellow, and his nephew used to say that he would one day be picked by mistake for a mushroom. His fellow-clerk in the office, and his accomplice in giggling and making giggle, was one strangely mated with him ; the strong, aspiring and un-scrupulous Thurlow, who, though fond of pleasure, was at the same time preparing himself to push his way to wealth and power. Cowper felt that Thurlow would reach the summit of ambition while he would himself remain below, and made his friend prom-ise when he was Chancellor to give him something. When Thurlow was Chancellor, he gave Cowper his advice on translating Homer.

At the end of his three years with the attorney, Cowper took chambers in the Middle, from which he afterwards removed to the Inner Temple. The Temple is now a pile of law offices. In those days it was still a Society. One of Cowper's set says of it : "The Temple is the barrier that divides the City and Suburbs ; and the gentlemen who reside there seem influenced by the situa-tion of the place they inhabit. Templars are in general a kind of citizen courtiers. They aim at the air and the mien of the draw-ing-room, but the holy-day smoothness of a 'prentice, heightened with some additional touches of the rake or coxcomb, betrays it-self in everything they do. The Temple, however, is stocked with its peculiar beaux, wits, poets, critics, and every character in the gay world ; and it is a thousand pities that so pretty a society should be disgraced with a few dull fellows, who can submit to puzzle them-

selves with cases and reports, and have not taste enough to follow
the genteel method of studying the law." Cowper, at all events,
studied law by the genteel method; he read it almost as little in
the Temple as he had in the attorney's office, though in due course
of time he was formally called to the Bar, and even managed in
some way to acquire a reputation which, when he had entirely
given up the profession, brought him a curious offer of a readership
at Lyons Inn. His time was given to literature, and he became a
member of a little circle of men of letters and journalists which had
its social centre in the Nonsense Club, consisting of seven Westminster men who dined together every Thursday. In the set were
Bonnell Thornton and Colman, twin wits; fellow-writers of the pe-
riodical essays which were the rage in that day; joint proprietors
of the *St. James's Chronicle;* contributors both of them to the
Connoisseur; and translators, Colman of Terence, Bonnell Thornton of Plautus, Colman being a dramatist besides. In the set was
Lloyd, another wit and essayist and a poet, with a character not of
the best. On the edge of the set, but apparently not in it, was
Churchill, who was then running a course which to many seemed
meteoric, and of whose verse, sometimes strong but always tur-
bid, Cowper conceived and retained an extravagant admiration.
Churchill was a link to Wilkes; Hogarth, too, was an ally of Colman, and helped him in his exhibition of Signs. The set was strictly confined to Westminsters. Gray and Mason, being Etonians,
were objects of its literary hostility, and butts of its satire. It is
needless to say much about these literary companions of Cowper's
youth; his intercourse with them was totally broken off; and before he himself became a poet its effects had been obliterated by
madness, entire change of mind, and the lapse of twenty years. If
a trace remained, it was in his admiration of Churchill's verses,
and in the general results of literary society, and of early practice
in composition. Cowper contributed to the *Connoisser* and the
St. James's Chronicle. His papers in the *Connoisseur* have been
preserved; they are mainly imitations of the lighter papers of the
Spectator by a student who affects the man of the world. He also
dallied with poetry, writing verses to "Delia," and an epistle to
Lloyd. He had translated an elegy of Tibullus when he was four-
teen, and at Westminster he had written an imitation of Phillips's
Splendid Shilling, which, Southey says, shows his manner formed.
He helped his Cambridge brother, John Cowper, in a translation
of the *Heriade.* He kept up his classics, especially his Homer.
In his letters there are proofs of his familiarity with Rousseau.
Two or three ballads which he wrote are lost, but he says they were
popular, and we may believe him. Probably they were patriotic.
'When poor Bob White," he says, "brought in the news of Bos-
cawen's success off the Coast of Portugal, how did I leap for joy!
When Hawke demolished Conflans, I was still more transported.
But nothing could express my rapture when Wolfe made the con-
quest of Quebec."

The "Delia" to whom Cowper wrote verses was his cousin

Theodora, with whom he had an unfortunate love affair. Her father, Ashley Cowper, forbade their marriage, nominally on the ground of consanguinity ; really, as Southey thinks, because he saw Cowper's unfitness for business, and inability to maintain a wife. Cowper felt the disappointment deeply at the time, as well he might do if Theodora resembled her sister, Lady Hesketh. Theodora remained unmarried, and, as we shall see, did not forget her lover. His letters she preserved till her death in extreme old age.

In 1756 Cowper's father died. There does not seem to have been much intercourse between them, nor does the son in after-years speak with any deep feeling of his loss : possibly his complaint in *Tirocinium* of the effect of boarding-schools, in estranging children from their parents, may have had some reference to his own case. His local affections, however, were very strong, and he felt with unusual keenness the final parting from his old home, and the pang of thinking that strangers usurp our dwelling and the familiar places will know us no more.

> " Where once we dwelt our name is heard no more,
> Children not thine have trod my nursery floor;
> And where the gardener Robin, day by day,
> Drew me to school along the public way,
> Delighted with my bauble coach, and wrapp'd
> In scarlet mantle warm and velvet capp'd.
> 'Tis now become a history little known,
> That once we call'd the pastoral house our own."

Before the rector's death, it seems, his pen had hardly realised the cruel frailty of the tenure by which a home in a parsonage is held. Of the family of Burkhampstead Rectory there was now left besides himself only his brother John Cowper, Fellow of Caius College, Cambridge, whose birth had cost their mother's life.

When Cowper was thirty-two, and still living in the Temple, came the sad and decisive crisis of his life. He went mad, and attempted suicide. What was the source of his madness? There is a vague tradition that it arose from licentiousness, which, no doubt, is sometimes the cause of insanity. But in Cowper's case there is no proof of anything of the kind : his confessions, after his conversion, of his own past sinfulness point to nothing worse than general ungodliness and occasional excess in wine ; and the tradition derives a colour of probability only from the loose lives of one or two of the wits and Bohemians with whom he had lived. His virtuous love of Theodora was scarcely compatible with low and gross amours. Generally, his madness is said to have been religious, and the blame is laid on the same foe to human weal as that of the sacrifice of Iphigenia. But when he first went mad, his conversion to Evangelicism had not taken place ; he had not led a particularly religious life, nor been greatly given to religious practices, though as a clergyman's son he naturally believed in religion, had at times felt religious emotions, and when he found his heart sinking had tried devotional books and prayers. The truth is, his

malady was simple hypochondria, having its source in delicacy of
constitution and weakness of digestion, combined with the influence
of melancholy surroundings. It had begun to attack him soon
after his settlement in his lonely chambers in the Temple, when his
pursuits and associations, as we have seen, were far from Evangelical. When its crisis arrived, he was living by himself without any
society of the kind that suited him (for the excitement of the Nonsense Club was sure to be followed by reaction); he had lost his
love, his father, his home, and, as it happened, also a dear friend ; his
little patrimony was fast dwindling away; he must have despaired
of success in his profession ; and his outlook was altogether dark.
It yielded to the remedies to which hypochondria usually yields—
air, exercise, sunshine, cheerful society, congenial occupation. It
came with January and went with May. Its gathering gloom was
dispelled for a time by a stroll in fine weather on the hills above
Southampton Water, and Cowper said that he was never unhappy
for a whole day in the company of Lady Hesketh. When he had
become a Methodist, his hypochondria took a religious form, but so
did his recovery from hypochondria : both must be set down to the
account of his faith, or neither. This double aspect of the matter
will plainly appear further on. A votary of wealth, when his brain
gives way under disease or age, fancies that he is a beggar. A
Methodist, when his brain gives way under the same influences,
fancies that he is forsaken of God. In both cases the root of the
malady is physical.

In the lines which Cowper sent on his disappointment to Theodora's sister, and which record the sources of his despondency, there
is not a touch of religious despair, or of anything connected with
religion. The catastrophe was brought on by an incident with
which religion had nothing to do. The office of clerk of the Journals in the House of Lords fell vacant, and was in the gift of Cowper's kinsman, Major Cowper, as patentee. Cowper received the
nomination. He had longed for the office sinfully, as he afterwards
fancied ; it would exactly have suited him, and made him comfortable for life. But his mind had by this time succumbed to his
malady. His fancy conjured up visions of opposition to the appointment in the House of Lords ; of hostility in the office where he
had to study the Journals ; of the terrors of an examination to be
undergone before the frowning peers. After hopelessly poring over
the Journals for some months he became quite mad, and his madness took a suicidal form. He has told with unsparing exactness
the story of his attempts to kill himself. In his youth his father
had unwisely given him a treatise in favour of suicide to read, and
when he argued against it, had listened to his reasonings in a si-
lence which he construed as sympathy with the writer, though it
seems to have been only unwillingness to think too badly of the
state of a departed friend. This now recurred to his mind, and
talk with casual companions in taverns and chop-houses was enough
in his present condition to confirm him in his belief that self-destruction was lawful. Evidently he was perfectly insane, for he

could not take up a newspaper without reading in it a fancied libel on himself. First he bought laudanum, and had gone out into the fields with the intention of swallowing it, when the love of life suggested another way of escaping the dreadful ordeal. He might sell all he had, fly to France, change his religion, and bury himself in a monastery. He went home to pack up ; but while he was looking over his portmanteau. his mood changed. and he again resolved on self-destruction. Taking a coach,·he ordered the coachman to drive to the Tower Wharf, intending to throw himself into the river. But the love of life once more interposed, under the guise of a low tide and a porter seated on the quay. Again in the coach, and afterwards in his chambers, he tried to swallow the laudanum ; but his hand was paralysed by "the convincing Spirit," aided by seasonable interruptions from the presence of his laundress and her husband, and at length he threw the laudanum away. On the night before the day appointed for the examination before the Lords, he lay some time with the point of his penknife pressed against his heart, but without courage to drive it home. Lastly, he tried to hang himself ; and on this occasion he seems to have been saved not by the love of life, or by want of resolution. but by mere accident. He had become insensible, when the garter by which he was suspended broke, and his fall brought in the laundress. who supposed him to be in a fit. He sent her to a friend, to whom he related all that had passed, and despatched him to his kinsman. His kinsman arrived, listened with horror to the story, made more vivid by the sight of the broken garter, saw at once that all thought of the appointment was at end, and carried away the instrument of nomination. Let those whom despondency assails read this passage of Cowper's life, and remember that he lived to write *John Gilpin* and *The Task.*

Cowper tells us that "to this moment he had felt no concern of a spiritual kind ; " that "ignorant of original sin, insensible of the guilt of actual transgression, he understood neither the Law nor the Gospel; the condemning nature of the one. nor the restoring mercies of the other." But after attempting suicide he was seized, as he well might be. with religious horrors. Now it was that he began to ask himself whether he had been guilty of the unpardonable sin, and was presently persuaded that he had, though it would be vain to inquire what he imagined the unpardonable sin to be. In this mood, he fancied that if there was any balm for him in Gilead, it would be found in the ministrations of his friend Martin Madan, an Evangelical clergyman of high repute, whom he had been wont to regard as an enthusiast. His Cambridge brother, John, the translator of the *Henriade*, seems to have had some philosophic doubts as to the efficacy of the proposed remedy ; but, like a philosopher, he consented to the experiment. Mr. Madan came and ministered, but in that distempered soul his balm turned to poison ; his religious conversations only fed the horrible illusion. A set of English Sapphics. written by Cowper at this time. and expressing his despair, were unfortunately preserved ; they are a ghastly play of the poetic faculty in a mind utterly deprived of self-control, and amidst the horrors of inrushing madness. Diabolical they might be termed more truly than religious.

There was nothing for it but a madhouse. The sufferer was consigned to the private asylum of Dr. Cotton, at St. Alban's. An ill-chosen physician Dr. Cotton would have been, if the malady had really had its source in religion; for he was himself a pious man, a writer of hymns, and was in the habit of holding religious intercourse with his patients. Cowper, after his recovery, speaks of that intercourse with the keenest pleasure and gratitude; so that, in the opinion of the two persons best qualified to judge, religion in this case was not the bane. Cowper has given us a full account of his recovery. It was brought about, as we can plainly see, by medical treatment wisely applied; but it came in the form of a burst of religious faith and hope. He rises one morning feeling better; grows cheerful over his breakfast, takes up the Bible, which in his fits of madness he always threw aside, and turns to a verse in the Epistle to the Romans. "Immediately I received strength to believe, and the full beams of the Sun of Righteousness shone upon me. I saw the sufficiency of the atonement He had made, my pardon in His blood, and the fulness and completeness of His justification. In a moment I believed and received the Gospel." Cotton at first mistrusted the sudden change; but he was at length satisfied, pronounced his patient cured, and discharged him from the asylum, after a detention of eighteen months. Cowper hymned his deliverance in *The Happy Change,* as in the hideous Sapphics he had given religious utterance to his despair.

> "The soul, a dreary province once
>   Of Satan's dark domain,
> Feels a new empire form'd within,
>   And owns a heavenly reign.

> "The glorious orb whose golden beams
>   The fruitful year control,
> Since first obedient to Thy word,
>   He started from the goal,

> "Has cheer'd the nations with the joys
>   His orient rays impart;
> But, Jesus, 'tis Thy light alone
>   Can shine upon the heart."

Once for all, the reader of Cowper's life must make up his mind to acquiesce in religious forms of expression. If he does not sympathise with them, he will recognise them as phenomena of opinion, and bear them like a philosopher. He can easily translate them into the language of psychology, or even of physiology, if he thinks fit.

CHAPTER II

THE storm was over; but it had swept away a great part of Cowper's scanty fortune, and almost all his friends. At thirty-five he was stranded and desolate. He was obliged to resign a Commissionership of Bankruptcy which he held, and little seems to have remained to him but the rent of his chambers in the Temple. A return to his profession was, of course, out of the question. His relations, however, combined to make up a little income for him, though from a hope of his family, he had become a melancholy disappointment; even the Major contributing, in spite of the rather trying incident of the nomination. His brother was kind, and did a brother's duty, but there does not seem to have been much sympathy between them; John Cowper did not become a convert to Evangelical doctrine till he was near his end, and he was incapable of sharing William's spiritual emotions. Of his brilliant companions, the Bonnell Thorntons and the Colmans, the quondam members of the Nonsense Club, he heard no more, till he had himself become famous. But he still had a staunch friend in a less brilliant member of the club, Joseph Hill, the lawyer, evidently a man who united strong sense and depth of character with literary tastes and love of fun, and who was throughout Cowper's life his Mentor in matters of business, with regard to which he was himself a child. He had brought with him from the asylum at St. Alban's the servant who had attended him there, and who had been drawn by the singular talisman of personal attraction which partly made up to this frail and helpless being for his entire lack of force. He had also brought from the same place an outcast boy whose case had excited his interest, and for whom he afterwards provided by putting him to a trade. The maintenance of these two retainers was expensive, and led to grumbling among the subscribers to the family subsidy, the Major especially threatening to withdraw his contribution. While the matter was in agitation, Cowper received an anonymous letter couched in the kindest terms, bidding him not distress himself, for that whatever deduction from his income might be made, the loss would be supplied by one who loved him tenderly and approved his conduct. In a letter to Lady Hesketh, he says that he wishes he knew who dictated this letter, and that he had seen not long before a style excessively like it. He can scarcely have failed to guess that it came from Theodora.

It is due to Cowper to say that he accepts the assistance of his relatives, and all acts of kindness done to him, with sweet and be-

coming thankfulness ; and that whatever dark fancies he may have
had about his religious state, when the evil spirit was upon him, he
always speaks with contentment and cheerfulness of his earthly
lot.   Nothing splenetic, no element of suspicious and irritable self-
love entered into the composition of his character.

On his release from the asylum he was taken in hand by his
brother John, who first tried to find lodgings for him at or near
Cambridge, and, failing in this, placed him at Huntingdon, within
a long ride, so that William becoming a horseman for the purpose,
the brothers could meet once a week.   Huntingdon was a quiet
little town with less than two thousand inhabitants, in a dull country, the best part of which was the Ouse, especially to Cowper, who
was fond of bathing.   Life there, as in other English country towns
in those days, and, indeed, till railroads made people everywhere
too restless and migratory for companionship, or even for acquaintance, was sociable in an unrefined way.   There were assemblies,
dances, races, card-parties, and a bowling-green, at which the little
world met and enjoyed itself.   From these the new convert, in his
spiritual ecstasy, of course turned away as mere modes of murdering time.   Three families received him with civility, two of them
with cordiality ; but the chief acquaintances he made were with
"odd scrambling fellows like himself ; " an eccentric water-drinker
and vegetarian who was to be met by early risers and walkers every
morning at six o'clock by his favourite spring ; a char-parson, of
the class common in those days of sinecurism and non-residence,
who walked sixteen miles every Sunday to serve two churches, besides reading daily prayers at Huntingdon, and who regaled his
friend with ale brewed by his own hands.   In his attached servant
the recluse boasted that he had a friend ; a friend he might have,
but hardly a companion.

For the first days, and even weeks, however, Huntingdon seemed
a paradise.   The heart of its new inhabitant was full of the unspeakable happiness that comes with calm after storm, with health
after the most terrible of maladies, with repose after the burning
fever of the brain.   When first he went to church, he was in a
spiritual ecstasy ; it was with difficulty that he restrained his emotions ; though his voice was silent, being stopped by the intensity
of his feelings, his heart within him sang for joy ; and when the
Gospel for the day was read, the sound of it was more than he
could well bear.   This brightness of his mind communicated itself
to all the objects round him—to the sluggish waters of the Ouse, to
dull. fenny Huntingdon, and to its commonplace inhabitants.

For about three months his cheerfulness lasted, and with the
help of books, and his rides to meet his brother, he got on pretty
well ; but then "the communion which he had so long been able
to maintain with the Lord was suddenly interrupted."   This is his
theological version of the case : the rationalistic version immediately follows : " I began to dislike my solitary situation, and to fear
I should never be able to weather out the winter in so lonely a
dwelling."   No man could be less fitted to bear a lonely life ; per-

sistence in the attempt would soon have brought back his madness. He was longing for a home : and a home was at hand to receive him. It was not, perhaps, one of the happiest kind ; but the influence which detracted from its advantages was the one which rendered it hospitable to the wanderer. If Christian piety was carried to a morbid excess beneath its roof, Christian charity opened its door.

The religious revival was now in full career, with Wesley for its chief apostle, organiser, and dictator : Whitefield for its great preacher; Fletcher of Madeley for its typical saint ; Lady Huntingdon for its patroness among the aristocracy, and the chief of its "devout women." From the pulpit, but still more from the stand of the field-preacher and through a well-trained army of social propagandists, it was assailing the scepticism, the coldness, the frivolity, the vices of the age. English society was deeply stirred : multitudes were converted, while among those who were not converted violent and sometimes cruel antagonism was aroused. The party had two wings—the Evangelicals. people of the wealthier class or clergymen of the Church of England, who remained within the Establishment; and the Methodists, people of the lower middle class or peasants, the personal converts and followers of Wesley and Whitefield, who. like their leaders, without a positive secession, soon found themselves organising a separate spiritual life in the freedom of Dissent. In the early stages of the movement the Evangelicals were to be counted at most by hundreds, the Methodists by hundreds of thousands. So far as the masses were concerned, it was, in fact, a preaching of Christianity anew. There was a cross division of the party into the Calvinists and those whom the Calvinists called Arminians ; Wesley belonging to the latter section, while the most pronounced and vehement of the Calvinists was "the fierce Toplady." As a rule, the darker and sterner element, that which delighted in religious terrors and threatenings was Calvinist, the milder and gentler, that which preached a gospel of love and hope continued to look up to Wesley, and to bear with him the reproach of being Arminian.

It is needless to enter into a minute description of Evangelicism and Methodism ; they are not things of the past. If Evangelicism has now been reduced to a narrow domain by the advancing forces of Ritualism on one side, and of Rationalism on the other, Methodism is still the great Protestant Church, especially beyond the Atlantic. The spiritual fire which they have kindled, the character which they have produced, the moral reforms which they have wrought. the works of charity and philanthropy to which they have given birth, are matters not only of recent memory, but of present experience. Like the great Protestant revivals which had preceded them in England, like the Moravian revival on the Continent, to which they were closely related, they sought to bring the soul into direct communion with its Maker. rejecting the intervention of a priesthood or a sacramental system. Unlike the previous revivals in England, they warred not against the rulers of the Church or

State, but only against vice or irreligion. Consequently, in the characters which they produced, as compared with those produced by Wycliffism, by the Reformation, and notably by Puritanism, there was less of force and the grandeur connected with it, more of gentleness, mysticism, and religious love. Even Quietism, or something like it, prevailed, especially among the Evangelicals, who were not like the Methodists, engaged in framing a new organisation or in wrestling with the barbarous vices of the lower order. No movement of the kind has ever been exempt from drawbacks and follies, from extravagance, exaggeration, breaches of good taste in religious matters, unctuousness, and cant—from chimerical attempts to get rid of the flesh and live an angelic life on earth—from delusions about special providences and miracles —from a tendency to overvalue doctrine and undervalue duty— from arrogant assumption of spiritual authority by leaders and preachers—from the self-righteousness which fancies itself the object of a divine election, and looks out with a sort of religious complacency from the Ark of Salvation in which it fancies itself securely placed, upon the drowning of an unregenerate world. Still, it will hardly be doubted that in the effects produced by Evangelicism and Methodism the good has outweighed the evil. Had Jansenism prospered as well, France might have had more of reform and less of revolution. The poet of the movement will not be condemned on account of his connexion with it, any more than Milton is condemned on account of his connexion with Puritanism, provided it be found that he also served art well.

Cowper, as we have seen, was already converted. In a letter written at this time to Lady Hesketh, he speaks of himself with great humility "as a convert made in Bedlam, who is more likely to be a stumbling-block to others than to advance their faith," though he adds, with reason enough, "that he who can ascribe an amendment of life and manners, and a reformation of the heart itself, to madness, is guilty of an absurdity that in any other case would fasten the imputation of madness upon himself." It is hence to be presumed that he traced his conversion to his spiritual intercourse with the Evangelical physician of St. Alban's, though the seed sown by Martin Madan may, perhaps, also have sprung up in his heart when the more propitious season arrived. However that may have been, the two great factors of Cowper's life were the malady which consigned him to poetic seclusion and the conversion to Evangelicism, which gave him his inspiration and his theme.

At Huntingdon dwelt the Rev. William Unwin, a clergyman, taking pupils, his wife, much younger than himself, and their son and daughter. It was a typical family of the Revival. Old Mr. Unwin is described by Cowper as a Parson Adams. The son, William Unwin, was preparing for holy orders. He was a man of some mark, and received tokens of intellectual respect from Paley, though he is best known as the friend to whom many of Cowper's letters are addressed. He it was who, struck by the appearance of the stranger, sought an opportunity of making his acquaintance

He found one, after morning church, when Cowper was taking his solitary walk beneath the trees. Under the influence of religious sympathy the acquaintance quickly ripened into friendship ; Cowper at once became one of the Unwin circle, and soon afterward, a vacancy being made by the departure of one of the pupils, he became a boarder in the house. This position he had passionately desired on religious grounds ; but in truth, he might well have desired it on economical grounds also, for he had begun to experience the difficulty and expensiveness, as well as the loneliness, of bachelor housekeeping, and financial deficit was evidently before him. To Mrs. Unwin he was from the first strongly drawn. " I met Mrs. Unwin in the street," he says, " and went home with her. She and I walked together near two hours in the garden, and had a conversation which did me more good than I should have received from an audience with the first prince in Europe. That woman is a blessing to me, and I never see her without being the better for her company." Mrs. Unwin's character is written in her portrait with its prim but pleasant features ; a Puritan and a precisian she was ; but she was not morose or sour, and she had a boundless capacity for affection. Lady Hesketh, a woman of the world, and a good judge in every respect, says of her at a later period, when she had passed with Cowper through many sad and trying years : " She is very far from grave ; on the contrary, she is cheerful and gay, and laughs *de bon cœur* upon the smallest provocation. Amidst all the little puritanical words which fall from her *de temps en temps,* she seems to have by nature a quiet fund of gaiety ; great indeed must it have been, not to have been wholly overcome by the close confinement in which she has lived, and the anxiety she must have undergone for one whom she certainly loves as well as one human being can love another. I will not say she idolizes him, because that she would think wrong : but she certainly seems to possess the truest regard and affection for this excellent creature, and, as I said before, has in the most literal sense of those words, no will or shadow of inclination but what is his. My account of Mrs. Unwin may seem, perhaps, to you, on comparing my letters, contradictory ; but when you consider that I began to write at the first moment that I saw her, you will not wonder. Her character develops itself by degrees ; and though I might lead you to suppose her grave and melancholy, she is not so by any means. When she speaks upon grave subjects, she does express herself with a puritanical tone, and in puritanical expressions, but on all subjects she seems to have a great disposition to cheerfulness and mirth ; and, indeed, had she not, she could not have gone through all she has. I must say, too, that she seems to be very well read in the English poets, as appears by several little quotations, which she makes from time to time, and has a true taste for what is excellent in that way."

When Cowper became an author he paid the highest respect to Mrs. Unwin as an instinctive critic, and called her his Lord Chamberlain, whose approbation was his sufficient licence for publication.

Life in the Unwin family is thus described by the new inmate :

—" As to amusements—I mean what the world calls such—we have none. The place, indeed, swarms with them ; and cards and dancing are the professed business of almost all the *gentle* inhabitants of Huntingdon. We refuse to take part in them, or to be accessories to this way of murdering our time, and by so doing have acquired the name of Methodists. Having told you how we *do not* spend our time, I will next say how we do. We breakfast commonly between eight and nine ; till eleven, we read either the Scripture, or the sermons of some faithful preacher of those holy mysteries ; at eleven we attend divine service, which is performed here twice every day ; and from twelve to three we separate, and amuse ourselves as we please. During that interval, I either read in my own apartment, or walk, or ride, or work in the garden. We seldom sit an hour after dinner, but if the weather permits, adjourn to the garden, where, with Mrs. Unwin and her son, I have generally the pleasure of religious conversation till tea-time. If it rains or is too windy for walking, we either converse within doors or sing some hymns of Martin's collection, and by the help of Mrs. Unwin's harpsichord make up a tolerable concert, in which our hearts, I hope, are the best performers. After tea we sally forth to walk in good earnest. Mrs. Unwin is a good walker, and we have generally travelled about four miles before we see home again. When the days are short we make this excursion in the former part of the day, between church time and dinner. At night we read and converse as before till supper, and commonly finish the evening either with hymns or a sermon, and last of all the family are called to prayers. I need not tell you that such a life as this is consistent with the utmost cheerfulness ; accordingly, we are all happy, and dwell together in unity as brethren."

Mrs. Cowper, the wife of Major (now Colonel) Cowper, to whom this was written, was herself strongly Evangelical ; Cowper had, in fact, unfortunately for him, turned from his other relations and friends to her on that account. She, therefore, would have no difficulty in thinking that such a life was consistent with cheerfulness, but ordinary readers will ask how it could fail to bring on another fit of hypochondria. The answer is probably to be found in the last words of the passage. Overstrained and ascetic piety found an antidote in affection. The Unwins were Puritans and enthusiasts, but their household was a picture of domestic love.

With the name of Mrs. Cowper is connected an incident which occurred at this time, and which illustrates the propensity to self-inspection and self-revelation which Cowper had in common with Rousseau. Huntingdon, like other little towns, was all eyes and gossip ; the new-comer was a mysterious stranger who kept himself aloof from the general society, and he naturally became the mark for a little stone-throwing. Young Unwin happening to be passing near " the Park " on his way from London to Huntingdon, Cowper gave him an introduction to its lady, in a letter to whom he afterwards disclosed his secret motive. " My dear Cousin,—You sent my friend Unwin home to us charmed with your kind reception of him, and with everything he saw at the Park. Shall I once more give you a peep into my vile and deceitful heart? What motive do you think lay at the bottom of my conduct when I desired him to call upon you? I did not suspect, at first, that pride and vainglory had any share in it; but quickly after I had recommended the visit to him, I discovered, in that fruitful soil, the very root of the matter. You know I am a stranger here; all such are suspected characters, unless they bring their credentials with them. To this moment, I believe, it is a matter of speculation in the place, whence I came, and to whom I belong. Though my friend, you may suppose, before I was admitted an inmate here, was satisfied that I was not a mere vagabond, and has, since that time, received more convincing proofs of my *sponsibility ;* yet I could not resist the opportunity of furnishing him with ocular demonstration of it, by introducing him to one of my most splendid connexions; that when he hears me called ' that fellow Cowper,' which has happened heretofore, he may be able, upon unquestionable evidence, to assert my gentlemanhood, and relieve me from the weight of that opprobrious appellation. Oh, pride! pride! it deceives with the subtlety of a serpent, and seems to walk erect, though it crawls upon the earth. How will it twist and twine itself about to get from under the Cross, which it is the glory of our Christian calling to be able to bear with patience and good-will. They who can guess at the heart of a stranger,—and you especially, who are of a compassionate temper,—will be more ready, perhaps, to excuse me, in this instance, than I can be to excuse myself. But, in good truth, it was abominable pride of heart, indignation, and vanity, and deserves no better name."

Once more, however obsolete Cowper's belief, and the language in which he expresses it may have become for many of us, we must take it as his philosophy of life. At this time, at all events, it was a source of happiness. "The storm being passed, a quiet and peaceful serenity of soul succeeded:" and the serenity in this case was unquestionably produced in part by faith.

> "I was a stricken deer that left the herd
> Long since; with many an arrow deep infixed
> My panting side was charged, when I withdrew
> To seek a tranquil death in distant shades.
> There was I found by one who had himself
> Been hurt by the archers. In his side he bore,
> And in his hands and feet, the cruel scars,
> With gentle force soliciting the darts,
> He drew them forth and healed and bade me live."

Cowper thought for a moment of taking orders, but his dread of appearing in public conspired with the good sense which lay beneath his excessive sensibility to put a veto on the design. He, however, exercised the zeal of a neophyte in proselytism to a greater extent than his own judgment and good taste approved when his enthusiasm had calmed down.

CHAPTER III.

AT OLNEY—MR. NEWTON.

COWPER had not been two years with the Unwins when Mr. Unwin, the father, was killed by a fall from his horse; this broke up the household. But between Cowper and Mrs. Unwin an indissoluble tie had been formed. It seems clear, notwithstanding Southey's assertion to the contrary, that they at one time meditated marriage, possibly as a propitiation to the evil tongues which did not spare even this most innocent connexion; but they were prevented from fulfilling their intention by a return of Cowper's malady. They became companions for life. Cowper says they were as mother and son to each other; but Mrs. Unwin was only seven years older than he. To label their connexion is impossible, and to try to do it would be a platitude. In his poems Cowper calls Mrs. Unwin Mary; she seems always to have called him Mr. Cowper. It is evident that her son, a strictly virtuous and religious man, never had the slightest misgiving about his mother's position.

The pair had to choose a dwelling-place : they chose Olney, in Buckinghamshire, on the Ouse. The Ouse was "a slow winding river," watering low meadows, from which crept pestilential fogs. Olney was a dull town, or rather village, inhabited by a population of lace-makers, ill-paid, fever-stricken, and for the most part as brutal as they were poor. There was not a woman in the place, excepting Mrs. Newton, with whom Mrs. Unwin could associate, or to whom she could look for help in sickness, or other need. The house in which the pair took up their abode was dismal, prison like, and tumble-down ; when they left it, the competitors for the succession were a cobbler and a publican. It looked upon the Market-place, but it was in the close neighbourhood of Silver End, the worst part of Olney. In winter the cellars were full of water. There were no pleasant walks within easy reach, and in winter Cowper's only exercise was pacing thirty yards of gravel, with the dreary supplement of dumb-bells. What was the attraction to this "well," this "abyss," as Cowper himself called it, and as, physically and socially, it was ?

The attraction was the presence of the Rev. John Newton, then curate of Olney. The vicar was Moses Brown, an Evangelical and a religious writer, who has even deserved a place among the worthies of the revival ; but a family of thirteen children, some of whom it appears too closely resembled the sons of Eli, had compelled him to take advantage of the indulgent character of the ecclesiastical polity of those days by becoming a pluralist and a non-resident, so that the curate had Olney to himself. The patron was the Lord Dartmouth, who, as Cowper says, "wore a coronet and prayed." John Newton was one of the shining lights and foremost leaders and preachers of the revival. His name was great both in the Evangelical churches within the pale of the Establishment, and in the Methodist churches without it. He was a brand plucked from the very heart of the burning. We have a memoir of his life, partly written by himself, in the form of letters, and completed under his superintendence. It is a monument of the age of Smollett and Wesley, not less characteristic than is Cellini's memoir of the times in which he lived. His father was master of a vessel, and took him to sea when he was eleven. His mother was a pious Dissenter, who was at great pains to store his mind with religious thoughts and pieces. She died when he was young, and his stepmother was not pious. He began to drag his religious anchor, and at length, having read Shaftesbury, left his theological moorings altogether, and drifted into a wide sea of ungodliness, blasphemy, and recklessness of living. Such at least is the picture drawn by the sinner saved of his own earlier years. While still but a stripling he fell desperately in love with a girl of thirteen; his affection for her was as constant as it was romantic; through all his wanderings and sufferings he never ceased to think of her, and after seven years she became his wife. His father frowned on the engagement, and he became estranged from home. He was impressed ; narrowly escaped shipwreck, deserted, and was arrested and flogged as a deserter. Released from the navy, he was taken into the service of a slave-dealer on the coast of Africa, at whose hands, and those of the man's negro mistress, he endured every sort of ill-treatment and contumely, being so starved that he was fain sometimes to devour raw roots to stay his hunger. His constitution must have been of iron to carry him through all that he endured. In the meantime his indomitable mind was engaged in attempts at self-culture ; he studied a Euclid which he had brought with him, drawing his diagrams on the sand ; and he afterwards managed to teach himself Latin by means of a Horace and a Latin Bible, aided by some slight vestiges of the education which he had received at a grammar school. His conversion was brought about by the continued influences of Thomas à Kempis, of a very narrow escape, after terrible sufferings, from shipwreck, of the impression made by the sights of the mighty deep on a soul which, in its weather-beaten casing, had retained its native sensibility, and, we may safely add, of the disregarded but not forgotten teachings of his pious mother. Providence was now kind to him ; he became captain of a slave-ship, and made several voyages on the business of trade. That it was a wicked trade he seems to have had no idea ; he says he never knew sweeter or more frequent hours of divine communion than on his two last voyages to Guinea. Afterwards it occurred to him that though his employment was genteel and profitable, it made him a sort of gaoler, unpleasantly conversant with both chains and shackles; and he besought Providence to fix him in a more humane calling.

In answer to his prayer came a fit of apoplexy, which made it dangerous for him to go to sea again. He obtained an office in the port of Liverpool, but soon he set his heart on becoming a minister of the Church of England. He applied for ordination to the Archbishop of York, but not having the degree required by the rules of the Establishment, he received through his Grace's secretary "the softest refusal imaginable." The Archbishop had not had the advantage of perusing Lord Macaulay's remarks on the difference between the policy of the Church of England and that of the Church of Rome, with regard to the utilization of religious enthusiasts. In the end Newton was ordained by the Bishop of Lincoln, and threw himself with the energy of a new-born apostle upon the irreligion and brutality of Olney. No Carthusian's breast could glow more intensely with the zeal which is the offspring of remorse. Newton was a Calvinist, of course, though it seems not an extreme one; otherwise he would probably have confirmed Cowper in the darkest of hallucinations. His religion was one of mystery and miracle, full of sudden conversions, special providences, and satanic visitations. He himself says that " his name was up about the country for preaching people mad;" it is true that in the eyes of the profane Methodism itself was madness; but he goes on to say "whether it is owing to the sedentary life the women live here, poring over their (lace) pillows for ten or twelve hours every day, and breathing confined air in their crowded little rooms, or whatever may be the immediate cause, I suppose we have near a dozen in different degrees disordered in their heads, and most of them I believe truly gracious people." He surmises that "these things are permitted in judgment, that they who seek occasion for cavilling and stumbling may have what they want." Nevertheless there were in him not only force, courage, burning zeal for doing good, but great kindness, and even tenderness of heart. " I see in this world," he said, "two heaps of human happiness and misery : now, if I can take but the smallest bit from one heap and add it to the other, I carry a point —if, as I go home, a child has dropped a half-penny, and by giving it another I can wipe away its tears, I feel I have done something." There was even in him a strain, if not of humour, of a shrewdness which was akin to it, and expressed itself in many pithy sayings. " If two angels came down from heaven to execute a divine command, and one was appointed to conduct an empire and the other to sweep a street in it, they would feel no inclination to change employments." " A Christian should never plead spirituality for being a sloven; if he be but a shoe-cleaner, he should be the best in the parish." " My principal method for defeating heresy is by establishing truth. One proposes to fill a bushel with tares; now if I can fill it first with wheat, I shall defy his attempts." That his

Calvinism was not very dark or sulphureous, seems to be shown from his repeating with gusto the saying of one of the old women of Olney when some preacher dwelt on the doctrine of predestination—" Ah, I have long settled that point; for if God had not chosen me before I was born, I am sure he would have seen nothing to have chosen me for afterwards." That he had too much sense to take mere profession for religion appears from his describing the Calvinists of Olney as of two sorts, which reminded him of the two baskets of Jeremiah's figs. The iron constitution which had carried him through so many hardships enabled him to continue in his ministry to extreme old age. A friend at length counselled him to stop before he found himself stopped by being able to speak no longer. " I cannot stop," he said, raising his voice. "What! shall the old African blasphemer stop while he can speak ? "

At the instance of a common friend, Newton had paid Mrs. Unwin a visit at Huntingdon, after her husband's death, and had at once established the ascendency of a powerful character over her and Cowper. He now beckoned the pair to his side, placed them in the house adjoining his own, and opened a private door between the two gardens, so as to have his spiritual children always beneath his eye. Under this, in the most essential respect, unhappy influence, Cowper and Mrs. Unwin together entered on "a decided course of Christian happiness:" that is to say, they spent all their days in a round of religious exercises without relaxation or relief. On fine summer evenings, as the sensible Lady Hesketh saw with dismay, instead of a walk, there was a prayer-meeting. Cowper himself was made to do violence to his intense shyness by leading in prayer. He was also made to visit the poor at once on spiritual missions, and on that of almsgiving, for which Thornton, the religious philanthropist, supplied Newton and his disciples with means. This, which Southey appears to think about the worst part of Newton's regimen, was probably its redeeming feature. The effect of doing good to others on any mind was sure to be good; and the sight of real suffering was likely to banish fancied ills. Cowper in this way gained, at all events, a practical knowledge of the poor, and learned to do them justice, though from a rather too theological point of view. Seclusion from the sinful world was as much a part of the system of Mr. Newton as it was of the system of Saint Benedict. Cowper was almost entirely cut off from intercourse with his friends and people of his own class. He dropped his correspondence even with his beloved cousin, Lady Hesketh, and would probably have dropped his correspondence with Hill, had not Hill's assistance in money matters been indispensable. To complete his mental isolation, it appears that, having sold his library, he had scarcely any books. Such a course of Christian happiness as this could only end in one way; and Newton himself seems to have had the sense to see that a storm was brewing, and that there was no way of conjuring it but by contriving some more congenial occupation. So the disciple was commanded to employ his poetical gifts in contributing to a hymn-book which Newton was compiling. Cowper's Olney hymns have not any serious value as poetry. Hymns rarely have. The relations of man with Deity transcend and repel poetical treatment. There is nothing in them on which the creative imagination can be exercised. Hymns can be little more than incense of the worshipping soul. Those of the Latin Church are the best; not because they are better poetry than the rest (for they are not), but because their language is the most sonorous. Cowper's hymns were accepted by the religious body for which they were written, as expressions of its spiritual feeling and desires; so far they were successful. They are the work of a religious man of culture, and free from anything wild, erotic, or unctuous. But, on the other hand, there is nothing in them suited to be the vehicle of lofty devotion; nothing, that we can conceive a multitude, or even a prayer-meeting, uplifting to heaven with voice and heart. Southey has pointed to some passages on which the shadow of the advancing malady falls; but in the main there is a predominance of religious joy and hope. The most despondent hymn of the series is *Temptation*, the thought of which resembles that of *The Castaway*.

Cowper's melancholy may have been aggravated by the loss of his only brother, who died about this time, and at whose death-bed he was present; though in the narrative which he wrote, joy at John's conversion and the religious happiness of his end seems to exclude the feelings by which hypochondria was likely to be fed. But his mode of life under Newton was enough to account for the return of his disease, which in this sense may be fairly laid to the charge of religion. He again went mad, fancied, as before, that he was rejected of Heaven, ceased to pray as one helplessly doomed, and again attempted suicide. Newton and Mrs. Unwin at first treated the disease as a diabolical visitation, and "with deplorable consistency," to borrow the phrase used by one of their friends in the case of Cowper's desperate abstinence from prayer, abstained from calling in a physician. Of this, again, their religion must bear the reproach. In other respects they behaved admirably. Mrs. Unwin, shut up for sixteen months with her unhappy partner, tended him with unfailing love; alone she did it, for he could bear no one else about him; though, to make her part more trying, he had conceived the insane idea that she hated him. Seldom has a stronger proof been given of the sustaining power of affection. Assuredly, of whatever Cowper may have afterwards done for his kind, a great part must be set down to the credit of Mrs. Unwin.

" Mary ! I want a lyre with other strings,
    Such aid from heaven as some have feigned they drew,
    An eloquence scarce given to mortals, new
And undebased by praise of meaner things,
That, ere through age or woe I shed my wings,
    I may record thy worth with honour due,
    In verse as musical as thou art true,
And that immortalises whom it sings.

> But thou hast little need.   There is a book
> By seraphs writ with beams of heavenly light,
> On which the eyes of God not rarely look,
> A chronicle of actions just and bright;
> There all thy deeds, my faithful Mary, shine,
> And, since thou own'st that praise, I spare thee mine."

Newton's friendship, too, was sorely tried.   In the midst of the malady the lunatic took it into his head to transfer himself from his own house to the Vicarage, which he obstinately refused to leave; and Newton bore this infliction for several months without repining, though he might well pray earnestly for his friend's deliverance.   "The Lord has numbered the days in which I am appointed to wait on him in this dark valley, and he has given us such a love to him, both as a believer and a friend, that I am not weary; but to be sure his deliverance would be to me one of the greatest blessings my thoughts can conceive."   Dr. Cotton was at last called in, and under his treatment, evidently directed against a bodily disease, Cowper was at length restored to sanity.

Newton once compared his own walk in the world to that 'of a physician going through Bedlam.   But he was not skilful in his treatment of the literally insane.   He thought to cajole Cowper out of his cherished horrors by calling his attention to a case resembling his own.   The case was that of Simon Browne, a Dissenter, who had conceived the idea that, being under the displeasure of Heaven, he had been entirely deprived of his rational being and left with merely his animal nature.   He had accordingly resigned his ministry, and employed himself in compiling a dictionary, which, he said, was doing nothing that could require a reasonable soul. He seems to have thought that theology fell under the same category, for he proceeded to write some theological treatises, which he dedicated to Queen Caroline. calling her Majesty's attention to the singularity of the authorship as the most remarkable phenomenon of her reign.   Cowper, however, instead of falling into the desired train of reasoning, and being led to suspect the existence of a similar illusion in himself, merely rejected the claim of the pretended rival in spiritual affliction, declaring his own case to be far the more deplorable of the two.

Before the decided course of Christian happiness had time again to culminate in madness, fortunately for Cowper, Newton left Olney for St. Mary Woolnoth.   He was driven away at last by a quarrel with his barbarous parishioners. the cause of which did him credit.   A fire broke out at Olney, and burnt a good many of its straw-thatched cottages.   Newton ascribed the extinction of the fire rather to prayer than water, but he took the lead in practical measures of relief, and tried to remove the earthly cause of such visitations by putting an end to bonfires and illuminations on the 5th of November.   Threatened with the loss of their Guy Fawkes, the barbarians rose upon him, and he had a narrow escape from their violence. We are reminded of the case of Cotton Mather, who, after being a leader in witch-burning, nearly sacrificed his life in combatting the fanaticism which opposed itself to the intro-duction of inoculation. Let it always be remembered that besides its theological side, the Revival had its philanthropic and moral side ; that it abolished the slave-trade, and at last slavery ; that it waged war, and effective war, under the standard of the gospel, upon masses of vice and brutality, which had been totally neglected by the torpor of the Establishment ; that among large classes of the people it was the great civilising agency of the time.

Newton was succeeded as curate of Olney by his disciple, and a man of somewhat the same cast of mind and character, Thomas Scott, the writer of the *Commentary on the Bible* and *The Force of Truth.* To Scott Cowper seems not to have greatly taken. He complains that, as a preacher, he is always scolding the congrega-tion. Perhaps Newton had foreseen that it would be so, for he specially commended the spiritual son whom he was leaving to the care of the Rev. William Bull, of the neighbouring town of New-port Pagnell, a dissenting minister, but a member of a spiritual connexion which did not stop at the line of demarcation between Nonconformity and the Establishment. To Bull Cowper did greatly take ; he extols him as "a Dissenter, but a liberal one," a man of letters and of genius, master of a fine imagination—or, rather, not master of it—and addresses him as *Carissime Taurorum.* It is rather singular that Newton should have given himself such a suc-cessor. Bull was a great smoker, and had made himself a cozy and .secluded nook in his garden for the enjoyment of his pipe. He was probably something of a spiritual as well as of a physical Quietist, for he set Cowper to translate the poetry of the great exponent of Quietism, Madame Guyon. The theme of all the pieces which Cowper has translated is the same—Divine Love and the raptures of the heart that enjoys it—the blissful union of the drop with the Ocean—the Evangelical Nirvana. If this line of thought was not altogether healthy, or conducive to the vigorous performance of practical duty, it was, at all events, better than the dark fancy of Reprobation. In his admiration of Madame Guyon, her translator showed his affinity, and that of Protestants of the same school, to Fénelon and the Evangelical element which has lurked in the Ro-man Catholic church since the days of Thomas à Kempis.

CHAPTER IV.

AUTHORSHIP—THE MORAL SATIRES.

SINCE his recovery, Cowper had been looking out for what he most needed,. a pleasant occupation. He tried drawing, carpentering, gardening. Of gardening he had always been fond; and he understood it, as shown by the loving though somewhat "stercoraceous" minuteness of some passages in *The Task*. A little greenhouse, used as a parlour in summer, where he sat surrounded by beauty and fragrance, and lulled by pleasant sounds, was another product of the same pursuit, and seems almost Elysian in that dull, dark life. He also found amusement in keeping tame hares, and he fancied that he had reconciled the hare to man and dog. His three tame hares are among the canonised pets of literature, and they were to his genius what "Sailor" was to the genius of Byron. But Mrs. Unwin, who had terrible reason for studying his case, saw that the thing most wanted was congenial employment for the mind, and she incited him to try his hand at poetry on a larger scale. He listened to her advice, and when he was nearly fifty years of age became a poet. He had acquired the faculty of verse-writing, as we have seen ; he had even to some extant formed his manner when he was young. Age must by this time have quenched his fire, and tamed his imagination, so that the didactic style would suit him best. In the length of the interval between his early poems and his great work he resembles Milton : but widely different in the two cases had been the current of the intervening years.

Poetry written late in life is of course, free from youthful crudity and extravagance. It also escapes the youthful tendency to imitation. Cowper's authorship is ushered in by Southey with a history of English poetry ; but this is hardly in place : Cowper had little connexion with anything before him. Even his knowledge of poetry was not great. In his youth he had read the great poets, and had studied Milton especially with the ardour of intense admiration. Nothing ever made him so angry as Johnson's Life of Milton. "Oh!" he cries, "I could thrash his old jacket till I made his pension jingle in his pocket." Churchill had made a great —far too great—an impression on him when he was a Templar. Of Churchill, if of anybody, he must be regarded as a follower, though only in his earlier and less successful poems. In expression he always regarded as a model the neat and gay simplicity of Prior. But so little had he kept up his reading of anything but sermons and hymns, that he learned for the first time from Johnson's Lives the existence of Collins. He is the offspring of the Religious Revival rather than of any school of art. His most important relation to any of his predecessors is, in fact, one of antagonism to the hard glitter of Pope.

In urging her companion to write poetry, Mrs. Unwin was on the right path; her puritanism led her astray in the choice of a theme. She suggested *The Progress of Error* as a subject for a " Móral Satire." It was unhappily adopted, and *The Progress of Error* was followed by *Truth, Table Talk, Expostulation, Hope, Charity, Conversation,* and *Retirement.* When the series was published, *Table Talk* was put first, being supposed to be the lightest and the most attractive to an unregenerate world. The judgment passed upon this set of poems at the time by the *Critical Review* seems blasphemous to the fond biographer, and is so devoid of modern smartness as to be almost interesting as a literary fossil. But it must be deemed essentially just, though the reviewer errs, as many reviewers have erred, in measuring the writer's capacity by the standard of his first performance. " These poems," said the *Critical Review,* " are written, as we learn from the title-page, by Mr. Cowper of the Inner Temple, who seems to be a man of a sober and religious turn of mind, with a benevolent heart, and a serious wish to inculcate the precepts of morality; he is not, however, possessed of any superior abilities or the power of genius requisite. for so arduous an undertaking. . . . . He says what is incontrovertible, and what has been said over and over again with much gravity, but says nothing new, sprightly, or entertaining; travelling on a plain, level, flat road, with great composure almost through the whole long and tedious volume, which is little better than a dull sermon in very indifferent verse on Truth, the Progress of Error, Charity, and some other grave subjects. If this author had followed the advice given by Caraccioli, and which he has chosen for one of the mottoes prefixed to these poems, he would have clothed his indisputable truths in some more becoming disguise, and rendered his work much more agreeable. In its present shape we cannot compliment him on its beauty; for as this bard himself sweetly sings :—

> " The clear harangue, and cold as it is clear,
> Falls soporific on the listless ear."

In justice to the bard it ought to be said that he wrote under the eye of the Rev. John Newton, to whom the design had been duly submitted, and who had given his *imprimatur* in the shape of a preface which took Johnson, the publisher, aback by its gravity. Newton would not have sanctioned any poetry which had not a distinctly religious object, and he received an assurance from the poet that the lively passages were introduced only as honey on the rim of the medicinal cup, to commend its healing contents to the lips of a giddy world. The Rev. John Newton must have been exceedingly austere if he thought that the quantity of honey used was excessive.

A genuine desire to make society better is always present in these poems, and its presence lends them the only interest which they possess except as historical monuments of a religious movement. Of satirical vigour they have scarcely a semblance. There are three kinds of satire, corresponding to as many different views of humanity and life; the Stoical, the Cynical, and the Epicurean. Of Stoical satire, with its strenuous hatred of vice and wrong, the type is Juvenal. Of Cynical satire, springing from bitter contempt of humanity, the type is Swift's Gulliver, while its quintessence is embodied in his lines on the Day of Judgment. Of Epicurean satire, flowing from a contempt of humanity which is not bitter, and lightly playing with the weakness and vanities of mankind, Horace is the classical example. To the first two kinds, Cowper's nature was totally alien, and when he attempts anything in either of those lines, the only result is a querulous and censorious acerbity, in which his real feelings had no part, and which on mature reflection offended his own better taste. In the Horatian kind he might have excelled, as the episode of the *Retired Statesman* in one of these poems shows. He might have excelled, that is, if like Horace he had known the world. But he did not know the world. He saw the "great Babel" only "through the loopholes of retreat," and in the columns of his weekly newspaper. Even during the years, long past, which he spent in the world, his experience had been confined to a small literary circle. Society was to him an abstraction on which he discoursed like a pulpiteer. His satiric whip not only has no lash, it is brandished in the air.

No man was ever less qualified for the office of a censor; his judgment is at once disarmed, and a breach in his principles is at once made by the slightest personal influence. Bishops are bad; they are like the Cretans, evil beasts and slow bellies; but the bishop whose brother Cowper knows is a blessing to the Church. Deans and Canons are lazy sinecurists, but there is a bright exception in the case of the Cowper who held a golden stall at Durham. Grinding India is criminal, but Warren Hastings is acacquitted, because he was with Cowper at Westminster. Discipline was deplorably relaxed in all colleges except that of which Cowper's brother was a fellow. Pluralities and resignation bonds, the grossest abuses of the Church, were perfectly defensible in the case of any friend or acquaintance of this Church Reformer. Bitter lines against Popery inserted in *The Task* were struck out, because the writer had made the acquaintance of Mr. and Mrs. Throckmorton, who were Roman Catholics. Smoking was detestable, except when practised by dear Mr. Bull. Even gambling, the blackest sin of fashionable society, is not to prevent Fox, the great Whig, from being a ruler in Israel. Besides, in all his social judgments, Cowper is at a wrong point of view. He is always de-luded by the idol of his cave. He writes perpetually on the twofold assumption that a life of retirement is more favourable to virtue than a life of action, and that " God made the country, while man made the town. Both parts of the assumption are untrue. A life of ac-tion is more favourable to virtue, as a rule, than a life of retirement, and the development of humanity is higher and richer, as a rule, in the town than in the country. If Cowper's retirement was virtuous, it was so because he was actively employed in the exercise of his highest faculties : had he been a mere idler, secluded from his kind, his retirement would not have been virtuous at all. His flight from the world was rendered necessary by his malady, and respectable by his literary work ; but it was a flight and not a victory. His misconception was fostered and partly produced by a religion which was essentially ascetic, and which, while it gave birth to characters of the highest and most energetic beneficence, represented salvation too little as the reward of effort, too much as the reward of passive belief and of spiritual emotion.

The most readable of the Moral Satires is *Retirement*, in which the writer is on his own ground, expressing his genuine feelings, and which is, in fact, a foretaste of *The Task*. *Expos-tulation*, a warning to England from the example of the Jews, is the best constructed ; the rest are totally wanting in unity, and even in connexion. In all there are flashes of epigrammatic smartness.

> " How shall I speak thee, or thy power address,
>   Thou God of our idolatry, the press ?
>   By thee, religion, liberty, and laws
>   Exert their influence, and advance their cause ;
>   By thee, worse plagues than Pharaoh's land befell,
>   Diffused, make earth the vestibule of hell :
>   Thou fountain, at which drink the good and wise,
>   Thou ever-bubbling spring of endless lies,
>   Like Eden's dread probationary tree,
>   Knowledge of good and evil is from thee."

Occasionally there are passages of higher merit. The episode of statesmen in *Retirement* has been already mentioned. The lines on the two disciples going to Emmaus in *Conversation*, though little more than a paraphrase of the Gospel narrative, convey pleasantly the Evangelical idea of the Divine Friend. Cowper says in one of his letters that he had been intimate with a man of fine taste who had confessed to him that though he could not subscribe to the truth of Christianity itself, he could never read this passage of St. Luke without being deeply affected by it, and feeling that if the stamp of divinity was impressed upon anything in the Scrip-tures, it was upon that passage.

> " It happen'd on a solemn eventide,
>   Soon after He that was our surety died,

Two bosom friends, each pensively inclined,
The scene of all those sorrows left behind,
Sought their own village, busied as they went
In musings worthy of the great event :
They spake of him they loved, of him whose life,
Though blameless, had incurr'd perpetual strife,
Whose deeds had left, in spite of hostile arts,
A deep memorial graven on their hearts.
The recollection, like a vein of ore,
The farther traced enrich'd them still the more ;
They thought him, and they justly thought him, one
Sent to do more than he appear'd to have done,
To exalt a people, and to place them high
Above all else, and wonder'd he should die.
Ere yet they brought their journey to an end,
A stranger join'd them, courteous as a friend,
And ask'd them with a kind engaging air
What their affliction was. and begg'd a share.
Inform'd, he gather'd up the broken thread,
And truth and wisdom gracing all he said,
Explain'd, illustrated, and search'd so well
The tender theme on which they chose to dwell,
That reaching home, the night, they said is near,
We must not now be parted, sojourn here.—
The new acquaintance soon became a guest,
And made so welcome at their simple feast,
He bless'd the bread, but vanish'd at the word,
And left them both exclaiming, 'Twas the Lord !
Did not our hearts feel all he deign'd to say,
Did they not burn within us by the way?"

The prude going to morning church in *Truth* is a good render-
ing of Hogarth's picture :—

"Yon ancient prude, whose wither'd features show
She might be young some forty years ago,
Her elbows pinion'd close upon her hips,
Her head erect, her fan upon her lips,
Her eyebrows arch'd, her eyes both gone astray
To watch yon amorous couple in their play,
With bony and unkerchief'd neck defies
The rude inclemency of wintry skies,
And sails with lappet-head and mincing airs
Daily, at clink of bell, to morning prayers.
To thrift and parsimony much inclined,
She yet allows herself that boy behind ;
The shivering urchin, bending as he goes,
With slipshod heels, and dew-drops at his nose,
His predecessor's coat advanced to wear,
Which future pages are yet doom'd to share ;
Carries her Bible tuck'd beneath his arm,
And hides his hands to keep his fingers warm."

Of personal allusions there are a few ; if the satirist had not
been prevented from indulging in them by his taste, he would

have been debarred by his ignorance. Lord Chesterfield, as the
incarnation of the world and the most brilliant servant of the
arch-enemy, comes in for a lashing under the name of Petronius.

> "Petronius! all the muses weep for thee,
> But every tear shall scald thy memory.
> The graces too, while virtue at their shrine
> Lay bleeding under that soft hand of thine,
> Felt each a mortal stab in her own breast,
> Abhorr'd the sacrifice, and cursed the priest.
> Thou polish'd and high-finish'd foe to truth,
> Gray-beard corrupter of our listening youth,
> To purge and skim away the filth of vice,
> That so refined it might the more entice,
> Then pour it on the morals of thy son
> To taint *his* heart, was worthy of *thine own*."

This is about the nearest approach to Juvenal that the Evangelical
satirist ever makes. In *Hope* there is a vehement vindication of
the memory of Whitefield. It is rather remarkable that there is
no mention of Wesley. But Cowper belonged to the Evangelical
rather than to the Methodist section. It may be doubted whether
the living Whitefield would have been much to his taste.

In the versification of the moral satires there are frequent
faults, especially in the earlier poems of the series; though Cowper's power of writing musical verse is attested both by the occasional poems and by *The Task.*

With the Moral Satires may be coupled, though written later,
Tirocinium ; or, a Review of Schools. Here Cowper has the advantage of treating a subject which he understood, about which he
felt strongly, and desired for a practical purpose to stir the feelings
of his readers. He set to work in bitter earnest. "There is a
sting," he says, "in verse that prose neither has nor can have;
and I do not know that schools in the gross, and especially public
schools, have ever been so pointedly condemned before. But they
are become a nuisance, a pest, an abomination, and it is fit that the
eyes and noses of mankind should be opened, if possible, to per-
ceive it." His descriptions of the miseries which children in his
day endured, and, in spite of all our improvements, must still to
some extent endure, in boarding-schools, and of the effects of the
system in estranging boys from their parents and deadening home
affections, are vivid and true. Of course, the Public School system was not to be overturned by rhyming, but the author of *Tirocinium* awakened attention to its faults, and probably did something towards amending them. The best lines, perhaps, have
been already quoted in connexion with the history of the writer's
boyhood. There are, however, other telling passages, such at that
on the indiscriminate use of emulation as a stimulus :—

> "Our public hives of puerile resort
> That are of chief and most approved report,

To such base hopes in many a sordid soul
Owe their repute in part, but not the whole.
A principle, whose proud pretensions pass
Unquestion'd, though the jewel be but glass,
That with a world not often over-nice
Ranks as a virtue, and is yet a vice,
Or rather a gross compound, justly tried,
Of envy, hatred, jealousy, and pride,
Contributes most perhaps to enhance their fame,
And Emulation is its precious name.
Boys once on fire with that contentious zeal
Feel all the rage that female rivals feel;
The prize of beauty in a woman's eyes
Not brighter than in theirs the scholar's prize.
The spirit of that competition burns
With all varieties of ill by turns,
Each vainly magnifies his own success,
Resents his fellow's, wishes it were less,
Exults in his miscarriage if he fail,
Deems his reward too great if he prevail,
And labors to surpass him day and night,
Less for improvement than to tickle spite.
The spur is powerful, and I grant its force;
It pricks the genius forward in its course,
Allows short time for play, and none for sloth,
And felt alike by each, advances both,
But judge where so much evil intervenes,
The end, though plausible, not worth the means.
Weigh, for a moment, classical desert
Against a heart depraved and temper hurt,
Hurt, too, perhaps for life, for early wrong
Done to the nobler part, affects it long,
And you are staunch indeed in learning's cause,
I you can crown a discipline that draws
Such mischiefs after it, with much applause."

He might have done more, if he had been able to point to the alternative of a good day-school, as a combination of home affections with the superior teachings hardly to be found, except in a large school, and which Cowper, in drawing his comparison between the two systems, fails to take into account.

To the same general class of poems belongs *Anti-Thelypthora*, which it is due to Cowper's memory to say was not published in his lifetime. It is an angry pasquinade on an absurd book advocating polygamy on Biblical grounds, by the Rev. Martin Madan, Cowper's quondam spiritual coünsellor. Alone among Cowper's works it has a taint of coarseness.

The Moral Satires pleased Franklin, to whom their social philosophy was congenial, as at a later day, in common with all Cowper's works, they pleased Cobden, who no doubt specially relished the passage in *Charity*, embodying the philanthropic sentiment of Free Trade. There was a trembling consultation as to the expediency of bringing the volume under the notice of Johnson. "One of his pointed sarcasms, if he should happen to be displeased, would soon find its way into all companies, and spoil the sale." " I think it would be well to send in our joint names, accompanied with a handsome card, such an one as you will know how to fabricate, and such as may predispose him to a favourable perusal of the book, by coaxing him into a good temper; for he is a great bear, with all his learning and penetration." Fear prevailed; but it seems that the book found its way into the dictator's hands, that his judgment on it was kind, and that he even did something to temper the wind of adverse criticism to the shorn lamb. Yet parts of it were likely to incur his displeasure as a Tory, as a Churchman, and as one who greatly preferred Fleet Street to the beauties of nature; while with the sentimental misery of the writer, he could have had no sympathy whatever. Of the incompleteness of Johnson's view of character there could be no better instance than the charming weakness of Cowper. Thurlow and Colman did not even acknowledge their copies, and were lashed for their breach of friendship with rather more vigour than the Moral Satires display, in *The Valedictory*, which unluckily survived for posthumous publication when the culprits had made their peace.

Cowper certainly misread himself if he believed that ambition, even literary ambition, was a large element in his character. But having published, he felt a keen interest in the success of his publication. Yet he took its failure and the adverse criticism very calmly. With all his sensitiveness, from irritable and suspicious egotism, such as is the most common cause of moral madness, he was singularly free. In this respect his philosophy served him well.

It may safely be said that the Moral Satires would have sunk into oblivion if they had not been buoyed up by *The Task*.

CHAPTER V.

THE TASK.

MRS. UNWIN'S influence produced the Moral Satires. *The Task* was born of a more potent inspiration. One day Mrs. Jones, the wife of a neighbouring clergyman, came into Olney to shop, and with her came her sister, Lady Austen, the widow of a Baronet, a woman of the world, who had lived much in France, gay, sparkling and vivacious, but at the same time full of feeling even to overflowing. The apparition acted like magic on the recluse. He desired Mrs. Unwin to ask the two ladies to stay to tea; then shrank from joining the party which he had himself invited; ended by joining it, and, his shyness giving way with a rush, engaged in animated conversation with Lady Austen, and walked with her part of the way home. On her an equally great effect appears to have been produced. A warm friendship at once sprang up, and before long Lady Austen had verses addressed to her as Sister Annie. Her ladyship, on her part, was smitten with a great love of retirement, and at the same time with great admiration for Mr. Scott, the curate of Olney, as a preacher, and she resolved to fit up for herself "that part of our great building which is at present occupied by Dick Coleman, his wife and child, and a thousand rats." That a woman of fashion, accustomed to French salons, should choose such an abode, with a pair of Puritans for her only society, seems to show that one of the Puritans at least must have possessed great powers of attraction. Better quarters were found for her in the Vicarage; and the private way between the gardens, which apparently had been closed since Newton's departure, was opened again.

Lady Austen's presence evidently wrought on Cowper like an elixir: "From a scene of the most uninterrupted retirement," he writes to Mrs. Unwin, "we have passed at once into a state of constant engagement. Not that our society is much multiplied; the addition of an individual has made all this difference. Lady Austen and we pass our days alternately at each other's Chateau. In the morning I walk with one or other of the ladies, and in the evening wind thread. Thus did Hercules, and thus probably did Samson, and thus do I; and, were both those heroes living, I should not fear to challenge them to a trial of skill in that business, or doubt to beat them both." It was, perhaps, while he was winding thread that Lady Austen told him the story of John Gilpin. He lay awake at night laughing over it, and next morning produced the ballad. It soon became famous, and was recited by Henderson, a popular actor, on the stage, though, as its gentility was doubtful, its author withheld his name. He afterwards fancied that this wonderful piece of humour had been written in a mood of the deepest depression. Probably he had written it in an interval of high spirits between two such moods. Moreover, he sometimes exaggerated his own misery. He will begin a letter with a _de profundis_, and towards the end forget his sorrows, glide into commonplace topics, and write about them in the ordinary strain. Lady Austen inspired _John Gilpin._ She inspired, it seems, the lines on the loss of the Royal George. She did more : she invited Cowper to try his hand at something considerable in blank verse. When he asked her for a subject, she was happier in her choice than the lady who had suggested the _Progress of Error._ She bade him take the sofa on which she was reclining, and which, sofas being then uncommon, was a more striking and suggestive object than it would be now. The right chord was struck; the subject was accepted ; and _The Sofa_ grew into _The Task;_ the title of the song reminding us that it was " commanded by the fair." As _Paradise Lost_ is to militant Puritanism, so is _The Task_ to the religious movement of its author's time. To its character as the poem. of a sect it no doubt owed and still owes much of its popularity. Not only did it give beautiful and effective expression to the sentiments of a large religious party, but it was about the only poetry that a strict Methodist or Evangelical could read; while to those whose worship was unritualistic and who were debarred by their principles from the theatre and the concert, anything in the way of art that was not illicit must have been eminently welcome. But _The Task_ has merits of a more universal and enduring kind. Its author himself says of it :—" If the work cannot boast a regular plan (in which respect, however, I do not think it altogether indefensible), it may yet boast that the reflections are naturally suggested always by the preceding passage, and that, except the fifth book, which is rather of a political aspect, the whole has one tendency, to discountenance the modern enthusiasm after a London life, and to recommend rural ease and leisure as friendly to the cause of piety and virtue." A regular plan, assuredly, _The Task_ has not. It rambles through a vast variety of subjects, religious, political, social, philosophical, and horticultural, with as little of method as its author used in taking his morning walks. Nor, as Mr. Benham has shown, are the reflections, as a rule, naturally suggested by the preceding passage. From the use of a sofa by the gouty to those who, being free from gout, do not need sofas—and so to country walks and country life, is hardly a natural transition. It is hardly a natural transition from the ice palace built by a Russian despot, to despotism and politics in general. But if Cowper deceives himself in fancying that there is a plan or a close connexion of parts, he is right as

to the existence of a pervading tendency. The praise of retirement and of country life as most friendly to piety and virtue, is the
perpetual refrain of *The Task*, if not its definite theme. From this
idea immediately flow the best and the most popular passages : those
which please apart from anything peculiar to a religious school;
those which keep the poem alive ; those which have found their way
into the heart of the nation, and intensified the taste for rural and
domestic happiness, to which they most winningly appeal. In these
Cowper pours out his inmostfeelings, with the liveliness of exhilara-
tion, enhanced by contrast with previous misery. The pleasures of
the country and of home—the walk, the garden, but above all the
"intimate delights " of the winter evening, the snug parlour, with its
close-drawn curtains shutting out the stormy night, the steaming and
bubbling tea-urn, the cheerful circle, the book read aloud, the newspaper through which we look out into the unquiet world—are
painted by the writer with a heartfelt enjoyment which infects
the reader. These are not the joys of a hero, nor are they the joys
of an Alcæus "singing amidst the clash of arms, or when he had
moored on the wet shore his storm-tost barque." But they are
pure joys, and they present themselves in competition with those
of Ranelagh and the Basset Table, which are not heroic or even
masculine, any more than they are pure.

The well-known passages at the opening of *The Winter Evening* are the self-portraiture of a soul in bliss—such bliss as that
soul could know—and the poet would have found it very difficult
to depict to himself by the utmost effort of his religious imagination
any paradise which he would really have enjoyed more.

> " Now stir the fire, and close the shutters fast.
> Let fall the curtains, wheel the sofa round,
> And while the bubbling and loud-hissing urn
> Throws up a steamy column, and the cups,
> That cheer but not inebriate, wait on eac
> So let us welcome peaceful evening in.
>
> * * * *
>
> This folio of four pages, happy work !
> Which not even critics criticise, that holds
> Inquisitive attention while I read
> Fast bound in chains of silence, which the fair,
> Though eloquent themselves, yet fear to break,
> What is it but a map of busy life,
> Its fluctuations and its vast concerns ?
>
> * * * *
>
> 'Tis pleasant through the loop-holes of retreat
> To peep at such a world. To see the stir
> Of the great Babel and not feel the crowd.
> To hear the roar she sends through all her gates
> At a safe distance, where the dying sound
> Falls a soft murmur on the injured ear.
> Thus sitting and surveying thus at ease
> The globe and its concerns, I seem advanced

To some secure and more than mortal height,
That liberates and exempts me from them all.
It turns submitted to my view, turns round
With all it generations; I behold
The tumult and am still. The sound of war
Has lost its terrors ere it reaches me,
Grieves but alarms me not. I mourn the pride
And avarice that make man a wolf to man,
Hear the faint echo of those brazen throats
By which he speaks the language of his heart,
And sigh, but never tremble at the sound.
He travels and expatiates, as the bee
From flower to flower, so he from land to land;
The manners, customs, policy of all
Pay contribution to the store he gleans;
He sucks intelligence in every clime,
And spreads the honey of his deep research
At his return, a rich repast for me.
He travels, and I too. I tread his deck,
Ascend his topmast, through his peering eyes
Discover countries, with a kindred heart
Suffer his woes and share in his escapes,
While fancy, like the finger of a clock,
Runs the great circuit, and is still at home.
    Oh, winter ! ruler of the inverted year,
Thy scatter'd hair with sleet like ashes fill'd,
Thy breath congeal'd upon thy lips, thy cheeks
Fringed with a beard made white with other snows
Than those of age; thy forehead wrapt in clouds
A leafless branch thy sceptre, and thy throne
A sliding car indebted to no wheels,
And urged by storms along its slippery way;
I love thee, all unlovely as thou seem'st,
And dreaded as thou art. Thou hold'st the sun
A prisoner in the yet undawning East,
Shortening his journey between morn and noon,
And hurrying him impatient of his stay
Down to the rosy West. But kindly still
Compensating his loss with added hours
Of social converse and instructive ease,
And gathering at short notice in one group
The family dispersed by daylight and its cares.
I crown thee king of intimate delights,
Fireside enjoyments, home-born happiness,
And all the comforts that the lowly roof
Of undisturb'd retirement, and the hours
Of long uninterrupted evening know."

The writer of *The Task* also deserves the crown which he has
himself claimed as a close observer and truthful painter of nature.
In this respect, he challenges comparison with Thomson. The
range of Thomson is far wider; he paints nature in all her moods,
Cowper only in a few, and those the gentlest, though he has said
of himself that "he was always an admirer of thunder-storms, even
before he knew whose voice he heard in them, but especially of

thunder rolling over the great waters." The great waters he had not seen for many years ; he had never, so far as we know, seen mountains, hardly even high hills ; his only landscape was the flat country watered by the Ouse. On the other hand, he is perfectly genuine, thoroughly English, entirely emancipated from false Arcadianism, the yoke of which still sits heavily upon Thomson, whose " muse " moreover, is perpetually " wafting " him away from the country and the climate which he knows to countries and climates which he does not know, and which he describes in the style of a prize poem. Cowper's landscapes, too, are peopled with the peasantry of England ; Thomson's, with Damons, Palæmons, and Musidoras, tricked out in the sentimental costume of the sham idyl. In Thomson, you always find the effort of the artist working up a description ; in Cowper, you find no effort ; the scene is simply mirrored on a mind of great sensibility and high pictorial power.

> " And witness, dear companion of my walks,
> Whose arm this twentieth winter I perceive
> Fast lock'd in mine, with pleasure such as love,
> Confirm'd by long experience of thy worth
> And well-tried virtues, could alone inspire—
> Witness a joy that thou hast doubled long.
> Thou know'st my praise of nature most sincere,
> And that my raptures are not conjured up
> To serve occasions of poetic pomp,
> But genuine, and art partner of them all.
> How oft upon yon eminence our pace
> Has slacken'd to a pause, and we have borne
> The ruffling wind, scarce conscious that it blew,
> While Admiration, feeding at the eye,
> And still unsated, dwelt upon the scene!
> Thence with what pleasure have we just discern
> The distant plough slow moving, and beside
> His labouring team that swerved not from the track,
> The sturdy swain diminish'd to a boy!
> Here Ouse, slow winding through a level plain
> Of spacious meads, with cattle sprinkled o'er,
> Conducts the eye along his sinuous course
> Delighted. There, fast rooted in their bank,
> Stand, never overlook'd, our favourite elms,
> That screen the herdsman's solitary hut ;
> While far beyond, and overthwart the stream,
> That, as with molten glass, inlays the vale,
> The sloping land recedes into the clouds ;
> Displaying on its varied side the grace
> Of hedge-row beauties numberless, square tower,
> Tall spire, from which the sound of cheerful bells
> Just undulates upon the listening ear,
> Groves, heaths, and smoking villages, remote.
> Scenes must be beautiful, which, daily viewed,
> Please daily, and whose novelty survives
> Long knowledge and the scrutiny of years—
> Praise justly due to those that I describe."

This is evidently genuine and spontaneous. We stand with Cowper and Mrs. Unwin on the hill in the ruffling wind, like them, scarcely conscious that it blows, and feed admiration at the eye upon the rich and thoroughly English champaign that is outspread below.

> " Nor rural sights alone, but rural sounds,
> Exhilarate the spirit, and restore
> The tone of languid Nature. Mighty winds,
> *That sweep the skirt of some far-spreading wood*
> *Of ancient growth, make music not unlike*
> *The dash of Ocean on his winding shore,*
> And lull the spirit while they fill the mind;
> Unnumber'd branches waving in the blast,
> And all their leaves fast fluttering, all at once.
> Nor less composure waits upon the roar
> Of distant floods, or on the softer voice
> Of neighbouring fountain, or of *rills that slip*
> *Through the cleft rock, and chiming as they fall*
> *Upon loose pebbles, lose themselves at length*
> *In matted grass that with a livelier green*
> *Betrays the secret of their silent course.*
> Nature inanimate employs sweet sounds,
> But animated nature sweeter still,
> To soothe and satisfy the human ear.
> Ten thousand warblers cheer the day, and one
> The livelong night : nor these alone, whose notes
> Nice-finger'd Art must emulate in vain,
> But cawing rooks, and kites that swim sublime
> In still-repeated circles, screaming loud,
> The jay, the pie, and e'en the boding owl
> That hails the rising moon, have charms for me.
> Sounds inharmonious in themselves and harsh,
> Yet heard in scenes where peace forever reigns,
> And only there, please highly for their sake."

Affection such as the last lines display for the inharmonious at well as the harmonious, for the uncomely as well as the comely parts of nature, has been made familiar by Wordsworth, but it was new in the time of Cowper. Let us compare a landscape painted by Pope in his Windsor forest, with the lines just quoted, and we shall see the difference between the art of Cowper and that of the Augustan age.

> " Here waving groves a checkered scene display,
> And part admit and part exclude the day,
> As some coy nymph her lover's warm address
> Not quite indulges, nor can quite repress.
> There interspersed in lawns and opening glades
> The trees arise that share each other's shades :
> Here in full light the russet plains extend,
> There wrapt in clouds the bluish hills ascend.
> E'en the wild heath displays her purple dyes,
> And midst the desert fruitful fields arise,
> That crowned with tufted trees and springing corn.
> Like verdant isles the sable waste adorn."

The low Berkshire hills wrapt in clouds on a sunny day ; a sable desert in the neighbourhood of Windsor; fruitful fields arising in it, and crowned with tufted trees and springing corn— evidently Pope saw all this, not on an eminence, in the ruffling wind, but in his study with his back to the window, and the Georgics or a translation of them before him.

Here, again, is a little picture of rural life from the *Winter Morning Walk.*

" The cattle mourn in corners, where the fence
Screens them, and seem half-petrified to sleep
In unrecumbent sadness. There they wait
Their wonted fodder ; not like hungering man,
Fretful if unsupplied; but silent, meek,
And patient of the slow-paced swain's delay.
He from the stack carves out the accustomed load.
Deep-plunging, and again deep plunging oft, •
His broad keen knife into the solid mass :
Smooth as a wall the upright remnant stands,
With such undeviating and even force
He severs it away : no needless care,
Lest storms should overset the leaning pile
Deciduous, or its own unbalanced weight.
Forth goes the woodman, leaving unconcern'd
The cheerful haunts of man ; to wield the axe
And drive the wedge in yonder forest drear,
From morn to eve, his solitary task.
Shaggy, and lean, and shrewd, with pointed ears ￢
And tail cropp'd short, half lurcher and half cur, ￨
His dog attends him.   Close behind his heel
Now creeps he slow ; and now, with many a frisk
Wide-scampering, snatches up the drifted snow
With ivory teeth, or ploughs it with his snout ;
Then shakes his powder'd coat and barks for joy.
Heedless of all his pranks, the sturdy churl
Moves right toward the mark ; nor stops for aught,
But now and then with pressure of his thumb
To adjust the fragrant charge of a short tube,
That fumes beneath his nose : the trailing cloud
Streams far behind him, scenting all the air."

The minutely faithful description of the man carving the load of hay out of the stack, and again those of the gambolling dog, and the woodman smoking his pipe with the steam of smoke trailing behind him, remind us of the touches of minute fidelity in Homer. The same may be said of many other passages.

" The sheepfold here
Pours out its fleecy tenants o'er the glebe.
At first, progressive as a stream they seek
The middle field ; but, scatter'd by degrees,
Each to his choice, soon whiten all the land.
There from the sun-burnt hay-field homeward **creeps**
The loaded wain ; while lighten'd of its charge,

The wain that meets it passes swiftly by ;
The boorish driver leaning o'er his team
Vociferous and impatient of delay."

A specimen of more imaginative and distinctly poetical description is the well-known passage on evening, in writing which Cowper would seem to have had Collins in his mind.

" Come, Evening, once again, season of peace ;
Return, sweet Evening, and continue long !
Methinks I see thee in the streaky west,
With matron-step slow-moving, while the Night
Treads on thy sweeping train; one hand employed
In letting fall the curtain of repose
On bird and beast, the other charged for man
With sweet oblivion of the cares of day :
Not sumptuously adorn'd, nor needing aid,
Like homely-featured Night, of clustering gems !
A star or two just twinkling on thy brow
Suffices thee ; save that the moon is thine
No less than hers, not worn indeed on high
With ostentatious pageantry, but set
With modest grandeur in thy purple zone,
Resplendent less, but of an ampler round."

Beyond this line Cowper does not go, and had no idea of going ; he never thinks of lending a soul to material nature as Wordsworth and Shelley do. He is the poetic counterpart of Gainsborough, as the great descriptive poets of a later and more spiritual day are the counterparts of Turner. We have said that Cowper's peasants are genuine as well as his landscape ; he might have been a more exquisite Crabbe if he had turned his mind that way, instead of writing sermons about a world which to him was little more than an abstraction, distorted, moreover, and discoloured by his religious asceticism.

" Poor, yet industrious, modest, quiet, neat,
Such claim compassion in a night like this,
And have a friend in every feeling heart.
Warm'd, while it lasts, by labour, all day long
They brave the season, and yet find at eve,
Ill clad, and fed but sparely, time to cool.
The frugal housewife trembles when she lights
Her scanty stock of brushwood, blazing clear,
But dying soon, like all terrestrial joys.
A few small embers left, she nurses well ;
And, while her infant race, with outspread hands
And crowded knees sit cowering o'er the sparks,
Retires, content to quake, so they be warm'd.
The man feels least, as more inured than she
To winter, and the current in his veins
More briskly moved by his severer toil ;
Yet he, too, finds his own distress in theirs.

The taper soon extinguish'd, which I saw
Dangled along at the cold finger's end
Just when the day declined ; and the brown loaf
Lodged on the shelf, half eaten without sauce
Of savoury cheese, or butter, costlier still :
Sleep seems their only refuge : for, alas !
Where penury is felt the thought is chained,
And sweet colloquial pleasures arc but few!
With all this thrift they thrive not.   All the care
Ingenious Parsimony takes, but just
Saves the small inventory, bed and stool,
Skillet, and old carved chest, from public sale.
They live, and live without extorted alms
From grudging hands: but other boast have nône
To soothe their honest pride that scorns to beg,
Nor comfort else, but in their mutual love."

Here we have the plain, unvarnished record of visitings among
the poor of Olney. The last two lines are simple truth as well as
the rest.

"In some passages, especially in the second book, you will observe me very satirical."   In the second book of *The Task* there
are some bitter things about the clergy ; and in the passage pour-
traying a fashionable preacher, there is a touch of satiric vigour,
or rather of that power of comic description which was one of the
writer's gifts.   But of Cowper as a satirist enough has been said.

"What there is of a religious cast in the volume I have thrown
towards the end of it, for two reasons ; first, that I might not revolt
the reader at his entrance ; and, secondly, that my best impressions
might be made last.   Were I to write as many volumes as Lope de
Vega or Voltaire, not one of them would be without this tincture.
If the world like it not, so much the worse for them.   I make all
the concessions I can, that I may please them, but I will not please
them at the expense of conscience."   The passages of *The Task*
penned by conscience, taken together, form a lamentably large proportion of the poem.   An ordinary reader can be carried through
them, if at all, only by his interest in the history of opinion, or by
the companionship of the writer, who is always present, as Walton
is in his Angler, as White is in his Selbourne.   Cowper, however,
even at his worst, is a highly cultivated Methodist : if he is sometimes enthusiastic, and possibly superstitious, he is never coarse
or unctuous.   He speaks with contempt of "the twang of the con-
venticle."   Even his enthusiasm had by this time been somewhat
tempered.   Just after his conversion he used to preach to everybody.   He had found out, as he tells us himself, that this was a
mistake, that "the pulpit was for preaching ; the garden, the parlour, and the walk abroad were for friendly and agreeable conversation."   It may have been his consciousness of a certain change
in himself that deterred him from taking Newton into his confidence
when we engaged upon *The Task*.   The worst passages are those
which betray a fanatical antipathy to natural science, especially
that in the third book (150-190).   The episode of the judgment

of Heaven on the young atheist Misagathus, in the sixth book, is also fanatical and repulsive.

Puritanism had come into violent collision with the temporal power, and had contracted a character fiercely political and revolutionary. Methodism fought only against unbelief, vice, and the coldness of the Establishment; it was in no way political, much less revolutionary; by the recoil from the atheism of the French Revolution, its leaders, including Wesley himself, were drawn rather to the Tory side. Cowper, we have said, always remained in principle what he had been born, a Whig, an unrevolutionary Whig, an "Old Whig," to adopt the phrase made canonical by Burke.

> " 'Tis liberty alone that gives the flower
> Of fleeting life its lustre and perfume,
> And we are weeds without it. All constraint
> Except what wisdom lays on evil men
> Is evil."

The sentiment of these lines, which were familiar and dear to Cobden, is tempered by judicious professions of loyalty to a king who rules in accordance with the law. At one time Cowper was inclined to regard the government of George III. as a repetition of that of Charles I., absolutist in the State and reactionary in the Church; but the progress of revolutionary opinions evidently increased his loyalty, as it did that of many other Whigs, to the good Tory king. We shall presently see, however, that the views of the French Revolution itself expressed in his letters are wonderfully rational, calm, and free from the political panic and the apocalyptic hallucination, both of which we should rather have expected to find in him. He describes himself to Newton as having seen, since his second attack of madness, "an extramundane character with reference to this globe, and though not a native of the moon, not made of the dust of this planet." The Evangelical party has remained down to the present day non-political, and in its own estimation extramundane, taking part in the affairs of the nation only when some religious object was directly in view. In speaking of the family of nations, an Evangelical poet is of course a preacher of peace and human brotherhood. He has even in some lines of *Charity*, which also were dear to Cobden, remarkably anticipated the sentiment of modern economists respecting the influence of free trade in making one nation of mankind. The passage is defaced by an atrociously bad simile :—

> " Again—the band of commerce was design'd,
> To associate all the branches of mankind,
> And if a boundless plenty be the robe,
> Trade is the golden girdle of the globe.
> Wise to promote whatever end he means,
> God opens fruitful Nature's various scenes,
> Each climate needs what other climes produce,
> And offers something to the general use ;

No land but listens to the common call,
And in return receives supply from all.
This genial intercourse and mutual aid
Cheers what were else an universal shade,
Calls Nature from her ivy-mantled den,
And softens human rock-work into men."

Now and then, however, in reading *The Task*, we come across a dash of warlike patriotism which, amidst the general philanthropy, surprises and offends the reader's palate, like the taste of garlic in our butter.

An innocent Epicurism, tempered by religious asceticism of a mild kind—such is the philosophy of *The Task*, and such the ideal embodied in the portrait of the happy man with which it concludes. Whatever may be said of the religious asceticism, the Epicurism required a corrective to redeem it from selfishness and guard it against self-deceit. This solitary was serving humanity in the best way he could, not by his prayers, as in one rather fanatical passage he suggests, but by his literary work; he had need also to remember that humanity was serving him. The newspaper through which he looks out so complacently into the great "Babel," has been printed in the great Babel itself, and brought by the poor postman, with his "spattered boots, strapped waist, and frozen locks," to the recluse sitting comfortably by his fireside. The "fragrant lymph" poured by "the fair" for their companion in his cosy seclusion, has been brought over the sea by the trader, who must encounter the moral dangers of a trader's life, as well as the perils of the stormy wave. It is delivered at the door by

"The waggoner who bears
The pelting brunt of the tempestuous night,
With half-shut eyes and puckered cheeks and teeth
Presented bare against the storm;"

and whose coarseness and callousness, as he whips his team, are the consequences of the hard calling in which he ministers to the recluse's pleasure and refinement. If town life has its evils, from the city comes all that makes retirement comfortable and civilised. Retirement without the city would have been bookless, and have fed on acorns.

Rousseau is conscious of the necessity of some such institution as slavery, by way of basis for his beautiful life according to nature. The celestial purity and felicity of St. Pierre's *Paul and Virginia* are sustained by the labour of two faithful slaves. A weak point of Cowper's philosophy, taken apart from his own saving activity as a poet, betrays itself in somewhat similar way.

"Or if the garden with its many cares
All well repaid demand him, he attends
The welcome call, conscious how much the hand
Of lubbard labour needs his watchful eye,

> Oft loitering lazily if not o'erseen ;
> Or misapplying his unskilful strength
> But much performs himself, *no works indeed*
> *That ask robust tough sinews bred to toil,*
> *Servile employ,* but such as may amuse,
> Not tire, demanding rather skill than force."

We are told in *The Task* that there is no sin in allowing our own happiness to be enhanced by contrast with the less happy condition of others : if we are doing our best to increase the happiness of others, there is none. Cowper, as we have said before, was doing this to the utmost of his limited capacity.

Both in the Moral Satires and in *The Task,* there are sweeping denunciations of amusements which we now justly deem innocent, and without which, or something equivalent to them, the wrinkles on the brow of care could not be smoothed, nor life preserved from dulness and moroseness.   There is fanaticism in this, no doubt ; but in justice to the Methodist as well as to the Puritan, let it be remembered that the stage, card parties, and even dancing, once had in them something from which even the most liberal morality might recoil.

In his writings generally, but especially in *The Task*, Cowper, besides being an apostle of virtuous retirement and evangelical piety, is, by his general tone, an apostle of sensibility. *The Task* is a perpetual protest not only against the fashionable vices and the irreligion but against the hardness of the world ; and in a world which worshipped Chesterfield the protest was not needless, nor was it ineffective.   Among the most tangible characteristics of this special sensibility is the tendency of its brimming love of human-kind to overflow upon animals ; and of this there are marked instances in some passages of *The Task.*

> " I would not enter on my list of friends
> (Though graced with polished manners and fine sense,
> Yet wanting sensibility) the man
> Who needlessly sets foot upon a worm. "

Of Cowper's sentimentalism (to use the word in a neutral sense), part flowed from his own temperament, part was Evangelical, but part belonged to an element which was European, which produced the *Nouvelle Heloise* and the *Sorrows of Werther*, and which was found among the Jacobins in sinister companionship with the cruel frenzy of the Revolution. Cowper shows us several times that he had been a reader of Rousseau, nor did he fail to produce in his time a measure of the same effect which Rousseau produced ; though there have been so many sentimentalists since, and the vein has been so much worked, that it is difficult to carry ourselves back in imagination to the day in which Parisian ladies could forego balls to read the *Nouvelle Heloise*, or the stony heart of people of the world could be melted by *The Task.*

In his versification, as in his descriptions, Cowper flattered himself that he imitated no one. But he manifestly imitates the softer passages of Milton, whose music he compares in a rapturous passage of one of his letters to that of a fine organ. To produce melody and variety, he, like Milton, avails himself fully of all the resources of a composite language. Blank verse confined to short Anglo-Saxon words is apt to strike the ear, not like the swell of an organ, but like the tinkle of a musical-box.

The Task made Cowper famous. He was told that he had sixty readers at the Hague alone. The interest of his relations and friends in him revived, and those of whom he had heard nothing for many years emulously renewed their connexion. Colman and Thurlow reopened their correspondence with him, Colman writing to him " like a brother." Disciples—young Mr. Rose, for instance—came to sit at his feet. Complimentary letters were sent to him, and poems submitted to his judgment. His portrait was taken by famous painters. Literary lion-hunters began to fix their eyes upon him. His renown spread even to Olney. The clerk of All Saints', Northampton, came over to ask him to write the verses annually appended to the bill of mortality for that parish. Cowper suggested that " there were several men of genius in Northampton, particularly Mr. Cox, the statuary, who, as everybody knew, was a first-rate maker of verses." " Alas ! " replied the clerk, " I have heretofore borrowed help from him, but he is a gentleman of so much reading that the people of our town cannot understand him." The compliment was irresistible, and for seven years the author of *The Task* wrote the mortuary verses for All Saints', Northampton. Amusement, not profit, was Cowper's aim ; he rather rashly gave away his copyright to his publisher, and his success does not seem to have brought him money in a direct way ; but it brought him a pension of 300*l*. in the end. In the meantime it brought him presents, and among them an annual gift of 50*l*. from an anonymous hand, the first instalment being accompanied by a pretty snuff-box ornamented with a picture of the three hares. From the gracefulness of the gift, Southey infers that it came from a woman, and he conjectures that the woman was Theodora.

CHAPTER VI.

SHORT POEMS AND TRANSLATIONS.

The Task was not quite finished when the influence which had inspired it was withdrawn. Among the little mysteries and scandals of literary history is the rupture between Cowper and Lady Austen. Soon after the commencement of their friendship there had been a "fracas," of which Cowper gives an account in a letter to William Unwin. "My letters have already apprised you of that close and intimate connexion that took place between the lady you visited in Queen Anne Street and us. Nothing could be more promising, though sudden in the commencement. She treated us with as much unreservedness' of communication, as if we had been in the same house and educated together. At her departure, she herself proposed a correspondence, and, because writing does not agree with your mother, proposed a correspondence with me. This sort of intercourse had not been long maintained before I discovered, by some slight intimations of it, that she had conceived displeasure at somewhat I had written, though I cannot now recollect it; conscious of none but the most upright, inoffensive intentions. I yet apologised for the passage in question, and the flaw was healed again. Our correspondence after this proceeded smoothly for a considerable time; but at length, having had repeated occasion to observe that she expressed a sort of romantic idea of our merits, and built such expectations of felicity upon our friendship, as we were sure that nothing human could possibly answer, I wrote to remind her that we were mortal, to recommend her not to think more highly of us than the subject would warrant, and intimating that when we embellish a creature with colors taken from our own fancy, and, so adorned, admire and praise it beyond its real merits, we make it an idol, and have nothing to expect in the end but that it will deceive our hopes, and that we shall derive nothing from it but a painful conviction of our error. Your mother heard me read the letter; she read it herself, and honoured it with her warm approbation. But it gave mortal offence; it received, indeed, an answer, but such an one as I could by no means reply to; and there ended (for it was impossible it should ever be renewed) a friendship that bid fair to be lasting; being formed with a woman whose seeming stability of temper, whose knowledge of the world and great experience of its folly, but, above all, whose sense of religion and seriousness of mind (for with all that gaiety she is a great thinker) induced us both, in spite of that cautious reserve that marked our characters, to trust her, to love and value her, and to open our hearts for her reception. It may be necessary to add that, by her own desire, I wrote to her under the assumed relation of a brother, and she to me as my sister. *Ceu fumus in auras.*" It is impossible to read this without suspecting that there was more of "romance" on one side than there was either of romance or of consciousness of the situation on the other. On that occasion the reconciliation, though "impossible," took place, the lady sending, by way of olive branch, a pair of ruffles, which it was known she had begun to work before the quarrel. The second rupture was final. Hayley, who treats the matter with sad solemnity, tells us that Cowper's letter of farewell to Lady Austen, as she assured him herself, was admirable, though unluckily, not being gratified by it at the time, she had thrown it into the fire. Cowper has himself given us, in a letter to Lady Hesketh, with reference to the final rupture, a version of the whole affair :—" There came a lady into this country, by name and title Lady Austen, the widow of the late Sir Robert Austen. At first she lived with her sister about a mile from Olney ; but in a few weeks took lodgings at the Vicarage here. Between the Vicarage and the back of our house are interposed our garden, an orchard, and the garden belonging to the Vicarage. She had lived much in France, was very sensible, and had infinite vivacity. She took a great liking to us, and we to her. She had been used to a great deal of company, and we, fearing that she would feel such a transition into silent retirement irksome, contrived to give her our agreeable company often. Becoming continually more and more intimate, a practice at length obtained of our dining with each other alternately every day, Sundays excepted. In order to facilitate our communication, we made doors in the two garden-walls aforesaid, by which means we consideraby shortened the way from one house to the other, and could meet when we pleased without entering the town at all—a measure the rather expedient, because the town is abominably dirty, and s,he kept no carriage. On her first settlement in our neighbourhood I made it my own particular business (for at that time I was not employed in writing, having published my first volume and not begun my second) to pay my *devoirs* to her ladyship every morning at eleven. Customs very soon became laws. I began *The Task*, for she was the lady who gave me the *Sofa* for a subject. Being once engaged in the work, I began to feel the inconvenience of my morning attendance. We had seldom breakfasted ourselves till ten ; and the intervening hour was all the time I could find in the whole day for writing, and occasionally it would happen that the half of that hour was all that I could secure for the purpose. But there was no remedy. Long usage had made that which was at first optional a point of good manners, and consequently of necessity, and I was forced to neglect *The Task* to attend upon the Muse who had inspired the subject. But she had ill-health, and before I had quite finished the work was obliged to repair to Bristol." Evidently this was not the whole account of the matter, or there would have been no need for a formal letter of farewell. We are very sorry to find the revered Mr. Alexander Knox saying, in his correspondence with Bishop Jebb, that he had a severer idea of Lady Austen than he should wish to put into writing for publication, and that he almost suspected she was a very artful woman. On the other hand, the unsentimental Mr. Scott is reported to have said, " Who can be surprised that two women should be continually in the society of one man and not quarrel, sooner or later, with each other?" Considering what Mrs. Unwin had been to Cowper, and what he had been to her, a little jealousy on her part would not have been highly criminal.' But, as Southey observes, we shall soon see two women continually in the society of this very man without quarrelling with each other. That Lady Austen's behaviour to Mrs. Unwin was in the highest degree affectionate, Cowper has himself assured us. Whatever the cause may have been, this bird of paradise, having alighted for a moment in Olney, took wing and was seen no more.

Her place as a companion was supplied, and more than supplied, by Lady Hesketh, like her a woman of the world, and almost as bright and vivacious, but with more sense and stability of character, and who, moreover, could be treated as a sister without any danger of misunderstanding. The renewal of the intercourse between Cowper and the merry and affectionate play-fellow of his early days, had been one of the best fruits borne to him by *The Task*, or perhaps we should rather say by *John Gilpin;* for on reading that ballad she first became aware that her cousin had emerged from the dark seclusion of his truly Christian happiness, and might again be capable of intercourse with her sunny nature. Full of real happiness for Cowper were her visits to Olney ; the announcement of her coming threw him into a trepidation of delight. And how was this new rival received by Mrs. Unwin ? " There is something," says Lady Hesketh, in a letter which has been already quoted, " truly affectionate and sincere in Mrs. Unwin's manner. No one can express more heartily than she does her joy to have me at Olney ; and as this must be for his sake, it is an additional proof of her regard and esteem for him." She could even cheerfully yield precedence in trifles, which is the greatest trial of all. " Our friend," says Lady Hesketh, " delights in a large table and a large chair. There are two of the latter comforts in my parlour. I am sorry to say that he and I always spread ourselves out in them, leaving poor Mrs. Unwin to find all the comfort she can in a small one, half as high again as ours, and considerably harder than marble. However, she protests it is what she likes, that she prefers a high chair to a low one, and a hard to a soft one ; and I hope she is sincere ; indeed, I am persuaded she is. She never gave the slightest reason for doubting her sincerity; so Mr. Scott's coarse theory of the " two women " falls to the ground ; though, as

Lady Hesketh was not Lady Austen, room is still left for the more delicate and interesting hypothesis.

By Lady Hesketh's care Cowper was at last taken out of the "well" at Olney and transferred, with his partner, to a house at Weston, a place in the neighbourhood, but on higher ground, more cheerful, and in better air. The house at Weston belonged to Mr. Throckmorton, of Weston Hall, with whom and Mrs. Throckmorton, Cowper had become so intimate that they were already his Mr. and Mrs. Frog. It is a proof of his freedom from fanatical bitterness that he was rather drawn to them by their being Roman Catholics, and having suffered rude treatment from the Protestant boors of the neighbourhood. Weston Hall had its grounds, with the colonnade of chestnuts, the "sportive light" of which still "dances" on the pages of *The Task;* with the Wilderness,—

> " Whose well-rolled walks,
> With curvature of slow and easy sweep,
> Deception innocent, give ample space
> To narrow bounds —"

with the Grove,—

> "Between the upright shafts of whose tall elms
> We may discern the thresher at his task,
> Thump after thump resounds the constant flail
> That seems to swing uncertain, and yet falls
> Full on the destined ear. Wide flies the chaff,
> The rustling straw sends up a fragrant mist
> Of atoms, sparkling in the noonday beam."

A pretty little vignette, which the threshing-machine has now made antique. There were ramblings, picnics, and little dinner-parties. Lady Hesketh kept a carriage. Gayhurst, the seat of Mr. Wright, was visited, as well as Weston Hall; the life of the lonely pair was fast becoming social. The Rev. John Newton was absent in the flesh, but he was present in the spirit, thanks to the tattle of Olney. To show that he was, he addressed to Mrs. Unwin a letter of remonstrance on the serious change which had taken place in the habits of his spiritual children. It was answered by her companion, who in repelling the censure mingles the dignity of self-respect with a just appreciation of the censor's motives, in a style which showed that although he was sometimes mad, he was not a fool.

Having succeeded in one great poem, Cowper thought of writing another, and several subjects were started—*The Mediterranean, The Four Ages of Man, Yardley Oak. The Mediterranean* would not have suited him well if it was to be treated historically, for of history he was even more ignorant than most of those who have had the benefit of a classical education, being capable of believing that the Latin element of our language had come in with the Roman conquest. Of the *Four Ages* he wrote a fragment. Of *Yardley Oak* he wrote the opening; it was, apparently, to have been a survey of the countries in connexion with an immemorial oak which stood in a neighbouring chace.   But he was forced to say that the mind of man was not a fountain but a cistern, and his was a broken one.   He had expended his stock of materials for a long poem in *The Task.*

These, the sunniest days of Cowper's life, however, gave birth to many of those short poems which are perhaps his best, certainly his most popular works, and which will probably keep his name alive when *The Task* is read only in extracts.   *The Loss of the Royal George, The Solitude of Alexander Selkirk, The Poplar Field, The Shrubbery,* the *Lines on a Young Lady,* and those *To Mary,* will hold their places forever in the treasury of English Lyrics.   In its humble way *The Needless Alarm* is one of the most perfect of human compositions.   Cowper had reason to complain of Æsop for having written his fables before him.   One great charm of these little pieces is their perfect spontaneity.   Many of them were never published ; and generally they have the air of being the simple effusions of the moment, gay or sad.   When Cowper was in good spirits his joy, intensified by sensibility and past suffering, played like a fountain of light on all the little incidents of his quiet life.   An ink-glass, a flatting mill, a halibut served up for dinner, the killing of a snake in the garden, the arrival of a friend wet after a journey, a cat shut up in a drawer, sufficed to elicit a little jet of poetical delight, the highest and brightest jet of being *John Gilpin.* Lady Austen's voice and touch still faintly live in two or three pieces which were written for her harpsichord.   Some of the short poems, on the other hand, are poured from the darker urn, and the finest of them all is the saddest.   There is no need of illustrations unless it be to call attention to a secondary quality less noticed than those of more importance.   That which used to be specially called " wit," the faculty of ingenious and unexpected combination, such as is shown in the similes of *Hudibras* was possessed by Cowper in large measure.

> " A friendship that in frequent fits
>   Of controversial rage emits
>   The sparks of disputation,
>   Like hand-in-hand insurance plates,
>   Most unavoidably creates
>   The thought of conflagration.

> " Some fickle creatures boast a soul
>   True as a needle to the pole,
>   Their humour yet so various—
>   They manifest their whole life through
>   The needle's deviations too,
>   Their love is so precarious.

> " The great and small but rarely meet
>   On terms of amity complete ;
>   Plebeians must surrender,
>   And yield so much to noble folk,
>   is combining fire with smoke,
>   Obscurity with splendour.

" Some are so placid and serene
(As Irish bogs are always green),
  They sleep secure from waking;
And are indeed a bog, that bears
Your unparticipated cares
  Unmoved and without quaking.

" Courtier and patriot cannot mix
  Their heterogeneous politics
    Without an effervescence,
Like that of salts with lemon juice,
Which does not yet like that produce
    A friendly coalescence."

Faint presages of Byron are heard in such a poem as *The Shrub-bery;* and of Wordsworth in such a poem as that *To a Young Lady.* But of the lyrical depth and passion of the great Revolution poets Cowper is wholly devoid. His soul was stirred by no movement so mighty, if it were even capable of the impulse. Tenderness he has, and pathos as well as playfulness ;. has has unfailing grace and ease ; he has clearness like that of a trout-stream. Fashions, even our fashions, change. The more metaphysical poetry of our time has indeed too much in it, besides the metaphysics, to be in any danger of being ever laid on the shelf with the once admired conceits of Cowley ; yet it may one day in part lose, while the easier and more limpid kind of poetry may in part regain, its charm.

The opponents of the Slave Trade tried to enlist this winning voice in the service of their cause. Cowper disliked the task, but he wrote two or three anti-Slave-Trade ballads. *The Slave Trader in the Dumps,* with its ghastly array of horrors dancing a jig to a ballad metre, justifies the shrinking of an artist from a subject hardly fit for art.

If the cistern which had supplied *The Task* was exhausted, the rill of occasional poems still ran freely, fed by a spring which, so long as life presented the most trivial object or incident, could not fail. Why did not Cowper go on writing these charming pieces, which he evidently produced with the greatest facility ? Instead of this, he took, under an evil star, to translating Homer. The translation of Homer into verse is the Polar Expedition of literature, always failing, yet still desperately renewed. Homer defies modern reproduction. His primeval simplicity is a dew of the dawn which can never be re-distilled. His primeval savagery is almost equally unpresentable. What civilized poet can don the barbarian sufficiently to revel, or seem to revel, in the ghastly details of carnage,in hideous wounds described with surgical gusto, in the butchery of captives in cold blood,or even in those particulars of the shambles and the spit which to the troubadour of barbarism seem as delightful as the images of the harvest and the vintage ? Poetry can be translated into poetry only by taking up the ideas of the original into the mind of the translator, which is very difficult when the translator and the original are separated by a gulf of thought and feeling, and when the gulf is very wide, becomes impossible. There is nothing for it in the case of Homer but a prose translation. Even in prose to find perfect equivalents for some of the Homeric phrases is not easy. Whatever the chronological date of the Homeric poems may be, their political and psychological date may be pretty well fixed. Politically they belong, as the episode of Thersites shows, to the rise of democracy and to its first collision with aristocracy, which Homer regards with the feelings of a bard who sang in aristocratic halls. Psychologically they belong to the time when, in ideas and language, the moral was just disengaging itself from the physical. In the wail of Andromache, for instance, *adinon epos,* which Pope improves into "sadly dear," and Cowper, with better taste at all events, renders "precious," is really semi-physical, and scarcely capable of exact translation. It belongs to an unreproducible past, like the fierce joy which, in the same wail, bursts from the savage woman in the midst of her desolation at the thought of the numbers whom her husband's hands had slain. Cowper had studied the Homeric poems thoroughly in his youth ; he knew them so well that he was able to translate them, not very incorrectly with only the help of a Clavis ; he understood their peculiar qualities as well as it was possible for a reader without the historic sense to do ; he had compared Pope's translation carefully with the original, and had decisively noted the defects which make it not a version of Homer, but a periwigged epic of the Augustan age. In his own translation he avoids Pope's faults, and he preserves at least the dignity of the original, while his command of language could never fail him, nor could he ever lack the guidance of good taste. But we well know where he will be at his best. We turn at once to such passages as the description of Calypso's Isle.

> " Alighting on Pieria, down he (Hermes) stooped
> To Ocean, and the billows lightly skimmed
> In form a sea-mew, such as in the bays
> Tremendous of the barren deep her food
> Seeking, dips oft in brine her ample wing.
> In such disguise o'er many a wave he rode,
> But reaching, now, that isle remote, forsook
> The azure deep, and at the spacious grove
> Where dwelt the amber-tressed nymph arrived
> Found her within. A fire on all the hearth
> Blazed sprightly, and, afar diffused, the scent
> Of smooth-split cedar and of cypress-wood
> Odorous, burning cheered the happy isle.
> She, busied at the loom and plying fast
> Her golden shuttle, with melodious voice
> Sat chanting there ; a grove on either side,
> Alder and poplar, and the redolent branch
> Wide-spread of cypress, skirted dark the cave
> Where many a bird of broadest pinion built
> Secure her nest, the owl, the kite, and daw,
> Long-tongued frequenters of the sandy shores.
> A garden vine luxuriant on all sides

> Mantled the spacious cavern, cluster-hung
> Profuse ; four fountains of serenest lymph,
> Their sinuous course pursuing side by side,
> Strayed all around, and everywhere appeared
> Meadows of softest verdure purpled o'er
> With violets ; it was a scene to fill
> A God from heaven with wonder and delight."

There are faults in this, and even blunders, notably in the natural history ; and " serenest lymph " is a sad departure from Homeric simplicity. Still, on the whole, the passage in the translation charms, and its charm is tolerably identical with that of the original. In more martial and stirring passages the failure is more signal, and here especially we feel that if Pope's rhyming couplets are sorry equivalents for the Homeric hexameter, blank verse is superior to them only in a negative way. The real equivalent, if any, is the romance metre of Scott, parts of whose poems, notably the last canto of *Marmion* and some passages in the *Lay of the Last Minstrel*, are about the most Homeric things in our language. Cowper brought such poetic gifts to his work that his failure might have deterred others from making the same hopeless attempt. But a failure his work is ; the translation is no more a counterpart of the original, than the Ouse creeping through its meadows is the counterpart of the Ægean rolling before a fresh wind and under a bright sun. Pope delights school-boys ; Cowper delights nobody, though, on the rare occasions when he is taken from the shelf, he commends himself, in a certain measure, to the taste and judgment of cultivated men.

In his translations of Horace, both those from the Satires and those from the Odes, Cowper succeeds far better. Horace requires in his translator little of the fire which Cowper lacked. In the Odes he requires grace, in the Satires urbanity and playfulness, all of which Cowper had in abundance. Moreover, Horace is separated from us by no intellectual gulf. He belongs to what Dr. Arnold called the modern period of ancient history. Nor is Cowper's translation of part of the eighth book of Virgil's Æneid bad, in spite of the heaviness of the blank verse. Virgil, like Horace, is within his intellectual range.

As though a translation of the whole of the Homeric poems had not been enough to bury his finer faculty, and prevent him from giving us any more of the minor poems, the publishers seduced him into undertaking an edition of Milton, which was to eclipse all its predecessors in splendour. Perhaps he may have been partly entrapped by a chivalrous desire to rescue his idol from the disparagement cast on it by the tasteless and illiberal Johnson. The project, after weighing on his mind and spirits for some time, was abandoned, leaving as its traces only translations of Milton's Latin poems, and a few notes on *Paradise Lost*, in which there is too much of religion, too little of art.

Lady Hesketh had her eye on the Laureateship, and probably

with that view persuaded her cousin to write loyal verses on the
recovery of George III.   He wrote the verses, but to the hint of
the Laureateship he said, " Heaven guard my brows from the wreath
you mention, whatever wreath beside may hereafter adorn them.
It would be a leaden extinguisher clapt on my genius, and I should
never more produce a line worth reading."   Besides, was he not
already the mortuary poet of All Saints, Northampton?

CHAPTER VII.

THE LETTERS.

SOUTHEY, no mean judge in such a matter, calls Cowper the best of English letter-writers. If the first place is shared with him by any one it is by Byron, rather than by Gray, whose letters are pieces of fine writing, addressed to literary men, or Horace Walpole, whose letters are memoirs, the English counterpart of St. Simon. The letters both of Gray and Walpole, are manifestly written for publication. Those of Cowper have the true epistolary charm. They are conversation, perfectly artless, and at the same time autobiography, perfectly genuine ; whereas all formal autobiography is cooked. They are the vehicles of the writer's thoughts and feelings, and the mirror of his life. We have the strongest proofs that they were not written for publication. In many of them there are outpourings of wretchedness which could not possibly have been intended for any heart but that to which they were addressed, while others contain medical details which no one would have thought of presenting to the public eye. Some, we know, were answers to letters received but a moment before ; and Southey says that the manuscripts are very free from erasures. Though Cowper kept a note-book for subjects, which no doubt were scarce with him, it is manifest that he did not premeditate. Grace of form he never lacks, but this was a part of his nature, improved by his classical training. The character and the thoughts presented are those of a recluse who was sometimes a hypochondriac; the life is life at Olney. But simple self-revelation is always interesting, and a garrulous playfulness with great happiness of expression can lend a certain charm even to things most trivial and commonplace. There is also a certain pleasure in being carried back to the quiet days before railways and telegraphs, when people passed their whole lives on the same spot, and life moved always in the same tranquil round. In truth, it is to such days that letter-writing, as a species of literature, belongs ; telegrams and postal cards have almost killed it now.

The large collection of Cowper's letters is probably seldom taken from the shelf ; and the " Elegant Extracts " select those letters which are most sententious, and therefore least characteristic. Two or three specimens of the other style may not be unwelcome

or needless as elements of a biographical sketch ; though specimens hardly do justice to a series of which the charm, such as it is,
is evenly diffused, not gathered into centres of brilliancy like Madam
de Sévigné's letter on the Orleans Marriage. Here is a letter
written in the highest spirits to Lady Hesketh.

" Olney, Feb. 9th, 1786.

"MY DEAREST COUSIN,—I have been impatient · to tell you
that I am impatient to see you again. Mrs. Unwin partakes with me
in all my feelings upon this subject, and longs also to see you. I
should have told you so by the last post, but have been so com-
pletely occupied by this tormenting specimen, that it was impossible
to do it. I sent the General a letter on Monday, that would distress and alarm him ; I sent him another yesterday, that will, I
hope, quiet him again. Johnson has apologised very civilly for the
multitude of his friend's strictures ; and his friend has promised to
confine himself in future to a comparison of me with the original,
so that, I doubt not, we shall jog on merrily together. And now,
my dear, let me tell you once more that your kindness in promising
us a visit has charmed us both. I shall see you again. I shall
hear your voice. We shall take walks together. I will show you
my prospects—the hovel, the alcove, the Ouse and its banks, everything that I have described. I anticipate the pleasure of those
days not very far distant, and feel a part of it at this moment. Talk
not of an inn ! Mention it not for your life ! We have never had
so many visitors but we could easily accommodate them all ; though
we have received Unwin, and his wife, and his sister, and his son
all at once. My dear, I will not let you come till the end of May,
or beginning of June, because before that time my greenhouse will
not be ready to receive us, and it is the only pleasant room belonging to us. When the plants go out, we go in. I line it with mats,
and spread the floor with mats ; and there you shall sit with a bed
of mignonette at your side, and a hedge of honeysuckles, roses,
and jasmine ; and I will make you a bouquet of myrtle every day.
Sooner than the time I mention the country will not be in complete
beauty.

" And I will tell you what you shall find at your first entrance.
Imprimis, as soon as you have entered the vestibule, if you cast a
look on either side of you, you shall see on the right hand a box of
my making. It is the box in which have been lodged all my hares,
and in which lodges Puss at present ; but he, poor fellow, is worn
out with age, and promises to die before you can see him. On the
right hand stands a cupboard, the work of the same author ; it was
once a dove-cage, but I transformed it. Opposite to you stands a
table, which I also made ; but a merciless servant having scrubbed
it until it became paralytic, it serves no purpose now but of orna-
ment ; and all my clean shoes stand under it. On the left hand, at
the further end of this superb vestibule, you will find the door of
the parlour, into which I will conduct you, and where I will introduce you to Mrs. Unwin, unless we should meet her before, and

where we will be as happy as the day is long. Order yourself, my cousin, to the Swan at Newport, and there you shall find me ready to conduct you to Olney.

"My dear, I have told Homer what you say about casks and urns, and have asked him whether he is sure that it is a cask in which Jupiter keeps his wine. He swears that it is a cask, and that it will never be anything better than a cask to eternity. So, if the god is content with it, we must even wonder at his taste, and be so too.

"Adieu! my dearest, dearest cousin. W. C."

Here, by way of contrast, is a letter written in the lowest spirits possible to Mr. Newton. It displays literary grace inalienable even in the depths of hypochondria. It also shows plainly the connexion of hypochondria with the weather. January was a month to the return of which the sufferer always looked forward with dread as a mysterious season of evil. It was a season, especially at Olney, of thick fog combined with bitter frosts. To Cowper this state of the atmosphere appeared the emblem of his mental state; we see in it the cause. At the close the letter slides from spiritual despair to the worsted-merchant, showing that, as we remarked before, the language of despondency had become habitual, and does not always flow from a soul really in the depths of woe.

To the Rev. John Newton.

"Jan. 13th, 1784.

"My dear Friend,—I too have taken leave of the old year, and parted with it just when you did, but with very different sentiments and feelings upon the occasion. I looked back upon all the passages and occurrences of it, as a traveller looks back upon a wilderness through which he has passed with weariness and sorrow of heart, reaping no other fruit of his labour than the poor consolation that, dreary as the desert was, he has left it all behind him. The traveller would find even this comfort considerably lessened if, as soon as he had passed one wilderness, another of equal length, and equally desolate, should expect him. In this particular, his experience and mine would exactly tally. I should rejoice, indeed, that the old year is over and gone, if I had not every reason to prophesy a new one similar to it.

"The new year is already old in my account. I am not, indeed, sufficiently second-sighted to be able to boast by anticipation an acquaintance with the events of it yet unborn, but rest convinced that, be they what they may, not one of them comes a messenger of good to me. If even death itself should be of the number, he is no friend of mine. It is an alleviation of the woes even of an unenlightened man, that he can wish for death, and indulge a hope, at least, that in death he shall find deliverance. But, loaded as my life is with despair, I have no such comfort as would result from a supposed probability of better things to come, were it once

5

ended. For, more unhappy than the traveller with whom I set out, pass through what difficulties I may, through whatever dangers and afflictions, I am not a whit nearer the home, unless a dungeon may be called so. This is no very agreeable theme; but in so great a dearth of subjects to write upon, and especially impressed as I am at this moment with a sense of my own condition, I could choose no other. The weather is an exact emblem of my mind in its present state. A thick fog envelopes everything, and at the same time it freezes intensely. You will tell me that this cold gloom will be succeeded by a cheerful spring, and endeavour to encourage me to hope for a spiritual change resembling it;—but it will be lost labour. Nature revives again; but a soul once slain lives no more. The hedge that has been apparently dead, is not so; it will burst into leaf and blossom at the appointed time; but no such time is appointed for the stake that stands in it. It is as dead as it seems, and will prove itself no dissembler. The latter end of next month will complete a period of eleven years in which I have spoken no other language. It is a long time for a man, whose eyes were once opened, to spend in darkness; long enough to make despair an inveterate habit; and such it is in me. My friends, I know, expect that I shall see yet again. They think it necessary to the existence of divine truth, that he who once had possession of it should never finally lose it. I admit the solidity of this reasoning in every case but my own. And why not in my own? For causes which to them it appears madness to allege, but which rest upon my mind with a weight of immovable conviction. If I am recoverable, why am I thus?—why crippled and made useless in the Church, just at that time of life when, my judgment and experience being matured, I might be most useful?—why cashiered and turned out of service, till, according to the course of nature, there is not life enough left in me to make amends for the years I have lost— till there is no reasonable hope left that the fruit can ever pay the expense of the fallow? I forestall the answer:—God's ways are mysterious, and He giveth no account of His matters—an answer that would serve my purpose as well as theirs to use it. There is a mystery in my destruction, and in time it shall be explained.

" I am glad you have found so much hidden treasure; and Mrs. Unwin desires me to tell you that you did her no more than justice in believing that she would rejoice in it. It is not easy to surmise the reason why the reverend doctor, your predecessor, concealed it. Being a subject of a free government, and I suppose full of the divinity most in fashion, he could not fear lest his riches should expose him to persecution. Nor can I suppose that he held it any disgrace for a dignitary of the Church to be wealthy, at a time when Churchmen in general spare no pains to become so. But the wisdom of some men has a droll sort of knavishness in it, much like that of a magpie, who hides what he finds with a deal of contrivance, merely for the pleasure of doing it.

" Mrs. Unwin is tolerably well. She wishes me to add that she shall be obliged to Mrs. Newton, if, when an opportunity offers, she will give the worsted-merchant a jog. We congratulate you that Eliza does not grow worse, which I know you expected would be the case in the course of the winter. Present our love to her. Remember us to Sally Johnson, and assure yourself that we remain as warmly as ever, Yours, W. C.

"M. U."

In the next specimen we shall see the faculty of imparting interest to the most trivial incident by the way of telling it. The incident in this case is one which also forms the subject of the little poem called *The Colubriad.*

To the Rev. William Unwin.

"Aug. 3rd, 1782.

"My dear Friend,—Entertaining some hope that Mr. Newton's next letter would furnish me with the means of satisfying your inquiry on the subject of Dr. Johnson's opinion, I have till now delayed my answer to your last; but the information is not yet come, Mr. Newton having intermitted a week more than usual since his last writing. When I receive it, favourable or not, it shall be communicated to you; but I am not very sanguine in my expectations from that quarter. Very learned and very critical heads are hard to please. He may, perhaps, treat me with levity for the sake of my subject and design, but the composition, I think, will hardly escape his censure. Though all doctors may not be of the same mind, there is one doctor at least, whom I have lately discovered, my professed admirer. He too, like Johnson, was with difficulty persuaded to read, having an aversion to all poetry except the *Night Thoughts;* which, on a certain occasion, when being confined on board a ship, he had no other employment, he got by heart. He was, however, prevailed upon, and read me several times over; so that if my volume had sailed with him, instead of Dr. Young's, I might, perhaps, have occupied that shelf in his memory which he then allotted to the Doctor : his name is Renny, and he lives at Newport Pagnel.

"It is a sort of paradox, but it is true : we are never more in danger than when we think ourselves most secure, nor in reality more secure than when we seem to be most in danger. Both sides of this apparent contradiction were lately verified in my experience. Passing from the greenhouse to the barn, I saw three kittens (for we have so many in our retinue) looking with fixed attention at something, which lay on the threshold of a door, coiled up. I took but little notice of then at first; but a loud hiss engaged me to attend more closely, when behold—a viper ! the largest I remember to have seen, rearing itself, darting its forked tongue, and ejaculating the aforementioned hiss at the nose of a kitten, almost in contact with his lips. I ran into the hall for a hoe with a long handle, with which I intended to assail him, and returning in a few seconds missed him: he was gone, and I feared had escaped me. Still, however, the kitten sat watching immovably upon the same spot. I concluded, therefore, that, sliding between the door and the threshold, he had found his way out of the garden into the yard. I went round immediately, and there found him in close conversation with the old cat, whose curiosity being excited by so novel an appearance, inclined her to pat his head repeatedly with her fore foot; with her claws, however, sheathed, and not in anger, but in the way of philosophical inquiry and examination. To prevent her falling a victim to so laudable an exercise of her talents, I interposed in a moment with the hoe, and performed an act of decapitation, which, though not immediately mortal, proved so in the end. Had he slid into the passages, where it is dark, or had he, when in the yard, met with no interruption from the cat, and secreted himself in any of the outhouses, it is hardly possible but that some of the family must have been bitten; he might have been trodden upon without being perceived, and have slipped away before the sufferer could have well distinguished what foe had wounded him. Three years ago we discovered one in the same place, which the barber slew with a trowel.

"Our proposed removal to Mr. Small's was, as you suppose, a jest, or rather a joco-serious matter. We never looked upon it as entirely feasible, yet we saw in it something so like practicability, that we did not esteem it altogether unworthy of our attention. It was one of those projects which people of lively imaginations play with, and admire for a few days, and then break in pieces. Lady Austen returned on Thursday from London, where she spent the last fortnight, and whither she was called by an unexpected opportunity to dispose of the remainder of her lease. She has now, therefore, no longer any connexion with the great city; she has none on earth whom she calls friends but us, and no house but at Olney. Her abode is to be at the Vicarage, where she has hired as much room as she wants, which she will embellish with her own furniture, and which she will occupy, as soon as the minister's wife has produced another child, which is expected to make its entry in October.

"Mr. Bull, a dissenting minister of Newport, a learned, ingenious, good-natured, pious friend of ours, who sometimes visits us, and whom we visited last week, has put into my hands three volumes of French poetry, composed by Madame Guyon;—a quietist, say you, and a fanatic; I will have nothing to do with her. It is very well, you are welcome to have nothing to do with her, but in the meantime her verse is the only French verse I ever read that I found agreeable; there is a neatness in it equal to that which we applaud with so much reason in the compositions of Prior. I have translated several of them, and shall proceed in my translations till I have filled a Lilliputian paper-book I happen to have by me, which, when filled, I shall present to Mr. Bull. He is her passionate admirer, rode twenty miles to see her picture in the house of a stranger, which stranger politely insisted on his acceptance of it, and it now hangs over his parlour chimney. It is a striking portrait, too characteristic not to be a strong resemblance, and were it encompassed with a glory, instead of being dressed in a nun's hood, might pass for the face of an angel.

"Our meadows are covered with a winter-flood in August; the rushes with which our bottomless chairs were to have been bottomed, and much hay, which was not carried, are gone down the river on a voyage to Ely, and it is even uncertain whether they will ever return. *Sic transit gloria mundi !*

"I am glad you have found a curate; may he answer! Am happy in Mrs. Bouverie's continued approbation; it is worth while to write for such a reader. Yours, W. C."

The power of imparting interest to commonplace incidents is so great that we read with a sort of excitement a minute account of the conversion of an old card-table into a writing and dining table, with the causes and consequences of that momentous event; curiosity having been first cunningly aroused by the suggestion that the clerical friend to whom the letter is addressed might, if the mystery were not explained, be haunted by it when he was getting into his pulpit, at which time, as he had told Cowper, perplexing questions were apt to come into his mind.

A man who lived by himself could have little but himself to write about. Yet in these letters there is hardly a touch of offensive egotism. Nor is there any querulousness, except that of religious despondency. From those weaknesses Cowper was free. Of his proneness to self-revelation we have had a specimen already.

The minor antiquities of the generations immediately preceding ours are becoming rare, as compared with those of remote ages, because nobody thinks it worth while to preserve them. It is almost as easy to get a personal memento of Priam or Nimrod as it is to get a harpsichord, a spinning-wheel, a tinder-box, or a scratch-back. An Egyptian wig is attainable, a wig of the Georgian era is hardly so, mnch less a tie of the Regency. So it is with the scenes of common life a century or two ago. They are being lost. because they were familiar. Here are two of them, however, which have limned themselves with the distinctness of the camera-obscura on the page of a chronicler of trifles.

To the Rev. John Newton.

Nov. 17th, 1783.

"My dear Friend.—The country around is much alarmed with apprehensions of fire. Two have happened since that of Olney. One at Hitchin, where the damage is said to amount to eleven thousand pounds; and another, at a place not far from Hitchin, of which I have not yet learnt the name. Letters have been dropped at Bedford, threatening to burn the town; and the inhabitants have been so intimidated as to have place a guard in many parts of it, several nights past. Since our conflagration here, we have sent two woman and a boy to the justice for depredation; S.R. for stealing a piece of beef, which, in her excuse, she said she intended to take care of. This lady, whom you well remember, escaped for want of evidence; not that evidence was wanting, but our men of Gotham judged it unnecessary to send it. With her went the woman I mentioned before, who, it seems, has made some sort of profession, but upon this occasion allowed herself a latitude of conduct rather inconsistent with it, having filled her apron with wearing-apparel, which she likewise intended to take care of. She would have gone to the county gaol, had William Raban, the baker's son, who prosecuted, insisted upon it; but he, good-naturedly, though I think weakly, interposed in her favour, and begged her off. The young gentleman who accompanied these fair ones is the junior son of Molly Boswell. He had stolen some iron-work, the property of Griggs the butcher. Being convicted, he was ordered to be whipped, which operation he underwent at the cart's tail, from the stone-house to the high arch, and back again. He seemed to show great fortitude, but it was all an imposition upon the public. The beadle, who performed it, had filled his left hand with yellow ochre, through which, after every stroke, he drew the lash of his whip, leaving the appearance of a wound upon the skin, but in reality not hurting him at all. This being perceived by Mr. Constable H., who followed the beadle, he applied his cane, without any such management or precaution, to the shoulders of the too merciful executioner. The scene immediately became more interesting. The beadle could by no means be prevailed upon to strike hard, which provoked the constable to strike harder; and this double flogging continued, till a lass of Silver-End, pitying the pitiful beadle thus suffering under the hands of the pitiless constable, joined the procession, and placing herself immediately behind the latter, seized him by his capillary club, and pulling him backwards by the same, slapped his face with a most Amazon fury. This concatenation of events has taken up more of my paper than I intended it should, but I could not forbear to inform you how the beadle thrashed the thief, the constable the beadle, and the lady the constable, and how the thief was the only person concerned who suffered nothing. Mr. Teedon has been here, and is gone again. He came to thank me for some left-off clothes. In answer to our inquiries after his health, he replied that he had a slow fever, which made him take all possible care not to inflame his blood. I admitted his prudence, but in his particular instance could not very clearly discern the need of it. Pump water will not heat him much; and, to speak a little in his own style, more inebriating fluids are to him, I fancy, not very attainable. He brought us news, the truth of which, however, I do not vouch for, that the town of Bedford was actually on fire yesterday, and the flames not extinguished when the bearer of the tidings left it.

"Swift observes, when he is giving his reasons why the preacher is elevated always above his hearers, that, let the crowd be as great as it will below there is always room enough overhead. If the French philosophers can carry their art of flying to the perfection they desire, the observation may be reversed, the crowd will be overhead, and they will have most room who stay below. I can assure you, however, upon my own experience, that this way of travelling is very delightful. I dreamt a night or two since that I drove myself through the upper regions in a balloon and pair, with the greatest ease and security. Having finished the tour I intended, I made a short turn, and with one flourish of my whip, descended; my horses prancing and curvetting with an infinite share of spirit, but without the least danger, either to me or my vehicle. The time, we may suppose, is at hand, and seems to be prognosticated by my dream, when these airy excursions will be universal, when judges will fly the circuit, and bishops their visitations; and when the tour of Europe will be performed with much greater speed, and with equal advantage, by all who travel merely for the sake of having it to say that they have made.

"I beg you will accept for yourself and yours our unfeigned love, and remember me affectionately to Mr. Bacon, when you see him. Yours, my dear friend,

"WM. COWPER."

TO THE REV. JOHN NEWTON.

"March 29th, 1784.

"MY DEAR FRIEND,—It being his Majesty's pleasure that I should yet have another opportunity to write before he dissolves the Parliament, I avail myself of it with all possible alacrity. I thank you for your last, which was not the less welcome for coming, like an extraordinary gazette, at a time when it was not expected.

"As when the sea is uncommonly agitated, the water finds its way into creeks and holes of rocks, which in its calmer state it never reaches, in like manner the effect of these turbulent times is felt even at Orchard Side, where, in general, we live as undisturbed by the political element as shrimps or cockles that have been accidentally deposited in some hollow beyond the water-mark, by the usual dashing of the waves. We were sitting yesterday after dinner, the two ladies and myself, very composedly, and without the least apprehension of any such intrusion in our snug parlour, one lady knitting, the other netting, and the gentleman winding worsted, when to our unspeakable surprise a mob appeared before the window: a smart rap was heard at the door, the boys bellowed, and the maid announced Mr. Grenville. Puss was unfortunately let out of her box, so that the candidate, with all his good friends at his heels, was refused admittance at the grand entry, and referred to the back door, as the only possible way of approach.

"Candidates are creatures not very susceptible of affronts, and would rather, I suppose, climb in at the window than be absolutely excluded. In a minute, the yard, the kitchen, and the parlour were filled. Mr. Grenville, advancing toward me, shook me by the hand with a degree of cordiality that was extremely seducing. As soon as he, and as many more as could find chairs, were seated, he began to open the intent of his visit. I told him I had no vote, for which he readily gave me credit. I assured him I had no influence, which he was not equally inclined to believe, and the less, no doubt, because Mr. Ashburner, the draper, addressing himself to me at this moment, informed me that I had a great deal. Supposing that I could not be possessed of such a treasure without knowing it, I ventured to confirm my first assertion by saying, that if I had any I was utterly at a loss to imagine where it could be, or wherein it consisted. Thus ended the conference. Mr. Grenville squeezed me by the hand again, kissed the ladies, and withdrew. He kissed, likewise, the maid in the kitchen, and seemed, upon the whole, a most loving, kissing, kind-hearted gentleman. He is very young, genteel, and handsome. He has a pair of very good eyes in his head, which not being sufficient as it should seem for the many nice and difficult purposes of a senator, he has a third also, which he suspended from his buttonhole. The boys halloo'd; the dogs barked; puss scampered; the hero, with his long train of obsequious followers, withdrew. We made ourselves very merry with the adventure, and in a short time settled into our former tranquility, never probably to be thus interrupted more. I thought myself, however, happy in being able to affirm truly that I had not that influence for which he sued; and which, had I been possessed of it, with my present views of the dispute between the Crown and the Commons, I must have refused him, for he is on the side of the former. It is comfortable to be of no consequence in a world where one cannot exercise any without disobliging somebody. The town, however, seems to be much at his service, and if he be equally successful throughout the country, he will undoubtedly gain his election. Mr. Ashburner, perhaps, was a little mortified, because it was evident that I owed the honour of this visit to his misrepresentation of my importance. But had he thought proper to assure Mr. Grenville that I had three heads, I should not, I suppose, have been bound to produce them.

"Mr. Scott, who you say was so much admired in your pulpit, would be equally admired in his own, at least by all capable judges, were he not so apt to be angry with his congregation. This hurt him, and had he the understanding and eloquence of Paul himself, would still hurt him. He seldom, hardly ever indeed, preaches a gentle, well-tempered sermon, but I hear it highly commended : but warmth of temper, indulged to a degree that may be called scolding, defeats the end of preaching. It is a misapplication of his powers, which it also cripples, and tears away his hearers. But he is a good man, and may perhaps outgrow it.

"Many thanks for the worsted, which is excellent. We are as well as a spring hardly less severe than the severest winter will give us leave to be. With our united love, we conclude ourselves yours and Mrs. Newton's affectionate and faithful,   W. C.
                                                                                  M. U."

In 1789 the French Revolution, advancing with thunder-tread, makes even the hermit of Weston look up for a moment from his translation of Homer, though he little dreamed that he, with his gentle philanthropy and sentimentalism, had anything to do with the great overturn of the social and political systems of the past. From time to time some crash of especial magnitude awakens a faint echo in the letters.

To Lady Hesketh.

"July 7th, 1790.

"Instead of beginning with the saffron-vested mourning to which Homer invites me, on a morning that has no saffron vest to boast, I shall begin with you. It is irksome to us both to wait so long as we must for you, but we are willing to hope that by a longer stay you will make us amends for all this tedious procrastination.

"Mrs. Unwin has made known her whole case to Mr. Gregson, whose opinion of it has been very consolatory to me; he says, indeed, it is a case perfectly out of the reach of all physical aid, but at the same time not at all dangerous. Constant pain is a sad grievance, whatever part is affected, and she is hardly ever free from an aching head, as well as an uneasy side; but patience is an anodyne of God's own preparation, and of that he gives her largely.

"The French who, like all lively folks, are extreme in everything, are such in their zeal for freedom; and if it were possible to make so noble a cause ridiculous, their manner of promoting it could not fail to do so. Princes and peers reduced to plain gentlemanship, and gentles reduced to a level with their own lackeys, are excesses of which they will repent hereafter. Differences of rank and subordination are, I believe, of God's appointment, and consequently essential to the well-being of society; but what we mean by fanaticism in religion is exactly that which animates their politics; and, unless time should sober them, they will, after all, be an unhappy people. Perhaps it deserves not much to be wondered at, that at their first escape from tyrannic shackles they should act extravagantly, and treat their kings as they have sometimes treated their idol. To these, however, they are reconciled in due time again, but their respect for monarchy is at an end. They want nothing now but a little English sobriety, and that they want extremely. I heartily wish them some wit in their anger, for it were great pity that so many millions should be miserable for want of it."

This, it will be admitted, is very moderate and unapocalyptic. Presently Monarchical Europe takes arms against the Revolution. But there are two political observers at least who see that Monarchical Europe is making a mistake—Kaunitz and Cowper. "The French," observes Cowper to Lady Hesketh in December, 1792, "are a vain and childish people, and conduct themselves on this grand occasion with a levity and extravagance nearly akin to madness; but it would have been better for Austria and Prussia to let them alone. All nations have a right to choose their own form of government, and the sovereignty of the people is a doctrine that evinces itself; for, whenever the people choose to be masters, they always are so, and none can hinder them. God grant that we may have no revolution here, but unless we have reform, we certainly shall. Depend upon it, my dear, the hour has come when power founded on patronage and corrupt majorities must govern this land no longer. Concessions, too, must be made to Dissenters of every denomination. They have a right to them—a right to all the privileges of Englishmen, and sooner or later, by fair means or by foul, they will have them." Even in 1793, though he expresses, as he well might, a cordial abhorrence of the doings of the French, he calls them not fiends, but "madcaps." He expresses the strongest indignation against the Tory mob which sacked Priestley's house at Birmingham, as he does, in justice be it said, against all manifestations of fanaticism. We cannot help sometimes wishing, as we read these passages in the letters, that their calmness and reasonableness could have been communicated to another "Old Whig," who was setting the world on fire with his anti-revolutionary rhetoric.

It is true, as has already been said, that Cowper was "extramundane;" and that his political reasonableness was in part the result of the fancy that he and his fellow-saints had nothing to do with the world but to keep themselves clear of it, and let it go its own way to destruction. But it must also be admitted that while the wealth of Establishments of which Burke was the ardent defender, is necessarily reactionary in the highest degree, the tendency of religion itself, where it is genuine and sincere, must be to repress any selfish feeling about class or position, and to make men, in temporal matters, more willing to sacrifice the present to the future, especially where the hope is held out of moral as well as of material improvement. Thus it has come to pass that men who professed and imagined themselves to have no interest in this world have practically been its great reformers and improvers in the political and material as well as in the moral sphere.

The last specimen shall be one in the more sententious style, and one which proves that Cowper was capable of writing in a judicious manner on a difficult and delicate question—even a question so difficult and so delicate as that of the propriety of painting the face.

To the Rev. William Unwin.

"May 3d, 1784.

"My Dear Friend,—The subject of face painting may be considered, I think, in two points of view. First, there is room for dispute with respect to the consistency of the practice with good morals: and, secondly, whether it be, on the whole, convenient or not, may be a matter worthy of agitation. I set out with all the formality of logical disquisition, but do not promise to observe the same regularity any further than it may comport with my purpose of writing as fast as I can.

"As to the immorality of the custom, were I in France, I should see none. On the contrary, in seems in that country to be a symptom of modest consciousness, and a tacit confession of what all know to be true, that French faces have, in fact, neither red nor white of their own. This humble acknowledgment of a defect looks the more like a virtue, being found among a people not remarkable for humility. Again, before we can prove the practice to be immoral, we must prove immorality in the design of those who use it ; either that they intend a deception, or to kindle unlawful desires in the beholders. But the French ladies, so far as their purpose comes in question, must be acquitted of both these charges. Nobody supposes their colour to be natural for a moment, any more than he would if it were blue or green ; and this unambiguous judgment of the matter is owing to two causes : first, to the universal knowledge we have, that French women are naturally either brown or yellow, with very few exceptions ; and secondly, to the inartificial manner in which they paint ; for they do not, as I am most satisfactorily informed, even attempt an imitation of nature, but besmear themselves hastily, and at a venture, anxious only to lay on enough. Where, therefore, there is no wanton intention, nor a wish to deceive. I can discover no immorality. But in England. I am afraid our painted ladies are not clearly entitled to the same apology. They even imitate nature with such exactness that the whole public is sometimes divided into parties, who litigate with great warmth the question whether painted or not ? This was remarkably the case with a Miss B——, whom I well remember. Her roses and lilies were never discovered to be spurious till she attained an age that made the supposition of their being natural impossible. This anxiety to be not merely red and white, which is all they aim at in France. but to be thought very beautiful, and much more beautiful than Nature has made them, is a symptom not very favourable to the idea we would wish to entertain of the chastity, purity, and modesty of our countrywomen. That they are guilty of a design to deceive, is certain. Otherwise why so much art? and if to deceive, wherefore and with what purpose ? Certainly either to gratify vanity of the silliest kind, or, which is still more criminal, to decoy and enveigle, and carry on more successfully the business of temptation. Here, therefore, my opinion splits itself into two opposite sides upon the same question. I can suppose a French woman, though painted an inch deep, to be a virtuous, discreet, excellent character ; and in no instance should I think the worse of one because she was painted. But an English belle must pardon me if I have not the same charity for her. She is at least an impostor, whether she cheats me or not, because she means to do so ; and it is well if that be all the censure that she deserves.

" This brings me to my second class of ideas upon this topic : and here I feel that I should be fearfully puzzled were I called upon to recommend the practice on the score of convenience. If a husband chose that his wife should paint, perhaps it might be her duty, as well as her interest, to comply. But I think he would not much consult his own, for reasons that will follow. In the first place, she would admire herself the more ; and in the next, if she managed the matter well, she might be more admired by others ; an acquisition that might bring her virtue under trials, to which otherwise it might never have been exposed. In no other case, however can I imagine the practice in this country to be either expedient or convenient. As a general one it certainly is not ex-pedient, because, in general, English women have no occasion for it. A swarthy complexion is a rarity here ; and the sex, especially since inoculation has been so much in use, have very little cause to complain that nature has not been kind to them in the article of complexion. · They may hide and spoil a good one, but they cannot, at least they hardly can, give themselves a better. But even if they could, there is yet a tragedy in the sequel which should make them tremble.

" I understand that in France, though the use of rouge be gen-eral, the use of white paint is far from being so. In England, she that uses one commonly uses both. Now, all white paints, or lotions, or whatever they may be called, are mercurial ; consequently poisonous, consequently ruinous, in time, to the constitution. The Miss B —— above mentioned was a miserable witness of this truth it being certain that her flesh fell from her bones before she died. Lady Coventry was hardly a less melancholy proof of it ; and a London physician, perhaps, were he at liberty to blab, could publish a bill of female mortality, of a length that would astonish us.

" For these reasons I utterly condemn the practice, as it obtains in England ; and for a reason superior to all these, I must disap-prove of it. I cannot, indeed, discover that Scripture forbids it in so many words. But that anxious solicitude about the person, which such an artifice evidently betrays, is, I am sure, contrary to the tenor and spirit of it throughout. Show me a woman with a painted face, and I will show you a woman whose heart is set on things of the earth, and not on things above.

" But this observation of mine applies to it only when it is an imitative art. For, in the use of French women, I think it is as innocent as in the use of a wild Indian, who draws a circle round her face, and makes two spots, perhaps blue, perhaps white, in the middle of it. Such are my thoughts upon the matter.

" *Vive valeque.*

" Yours ever,

" W. C."

These letters have been chosen as illustrations of Cowper's epistolary style, and for that purpose they have been given entire. But they are also the best pictures of his character ; and his char-acter is everything. The events of his life worthy of record might all be comprised in a dozen pages.

CHAPTER VIII.

CLOSE OF LIFE.

COWPER says there could not have been a happier trio on earth than Lady Hesketh, Mrs. Unwin, and himself. Nevertheless, after his removal to Weston, he again went mad, and once more attempted self-destruction. His malady was constitutional, and it settled down upon him as his years increased, and his strength failed. He was now sixty. The Olney physicians, instead of husbanding his vital power, had wasted it away *secundum artem* by purging, bleeding, and emetics. He had overworked himself on his fatal translation of Homer, under the burden of which he moved, as he says himself, like an ass overladen with sand-bags. He had been getting up to work at six, and not breakfasting till eleven. And now the life from which his had for so many years been fed, itself began to fail. Mrs. Unwin was stricken with paralysis ; the stroke was slight, but of its nature there was no doubt. Her days of bodily life were numbered : of mental life there remained to her a still shorter span. Her excellent son, William Unwin, had died of a fever soon after the removal of the pair to Weston. He had been engaged in the work of his profession as a clergyman, and we do not hear of his being often at Olney. But he was in constant correspondence with Cowper, in whose heart as well as in that of Mrs. Unwin, his death must have left a great void, and his support was withdrawn just at the moment when it was about to become most necessary.

Happily, just at this juncture a new and a good friend appeared. Hayley was a mediocre poet, who had for a time obtained distinction above his merits. Afterwards his star had declined, but having an excellent heart, he had not been in the least soured by the downfall of his reputation. He was addicted to a pompous rotundity of style ; perhaps he was rather absurd ; but he was thoroughly good-natured, very anxious to make himself useful, and devoted to Cowper, to whom, as a poet, he looked up with an admiration unalloyed by any other feeling. Both of them, as it happened, were engaged on Milton, and an attempt had been made to set them by the ears ; but Hayley took advantage of it to introduce himself to Cowper with an effusion of the warmest esteem. He was at Weston when Mrs. Unwin was attacked with paralysis, and displayed his resource by trying to cure her with an electric-machine. At Eartham, on the coast of Sussex, he had, by an expenditure beyond his means, made for himself a little paradise, where it was his delight to gather a distinguished circle. To this place he gave the pair a pressing invitation, which was accepted in the vain hope that a change might do Mrs. Unwin good.

From Weston to Eartham was a three days' journey, an enterprise not undertaken without much trepidation and earnest prayer. It was safely accomplished, however, the enthusiastic Mr. Rose walking to meet his poet and philosopher on the way. Hayley had tried to get Thurlow to meet Cowper. A sojourn in a country house with the tremendous Thurlow, the only talker for whom Johnson condescended to prepare himself, would have been rather an overpowering pleasure ; and perhaps, after all, it was as well that Hayley could only get Cowper's disciple, Hurdis, afterwards professor of poetry at Oxford, and Charlotte Smith.

At Eartham, Cowper's portrait was painted by Romney.

> " Romney, expert infallibly to trace
> On chart or canvas not the form alone
> And semblance, but, however faintly shown
> The mind's impression too on every face,
> With strokes that time ought never to erase,
> Thou hast so pencilled mine that though I own
> The subject worthless, I have never known
> The artist shining with superior grace ;
> But this I mark, that symptoms none of woe
> In thy incomparable work appear :
> Well : I am satisfied it should be so,
> Since on maturer thought the cause is clear ;
> For in my looks what sorrow could'st thou see
> When I was Hayley's guest and sat to thee."

Southey observes that it was likely enough there would be no melancholy in the portrait, but that Hayley and Romney fell into a singular error in mistaking for "the light of genius" what Leigh Hunt calls "a fire fiercer than that either of intellect or fancy, gleaming from the raised and protruded eye."

Hayley evidently did his utmost to make his guest happy. They spent the hours in literary chat, and compared notes about Milton. The first days were days of enjoyment. But soon the recluse began to long for his nook at Weston. Even the extensiveness of the view at Eartham made his mind ache, and increased his melancholy. To Weston the pair returned ; the paralytic, of course, none the better for her journey. Her mind as well as her body was now rapidly giving way. We quote as biography that which is too well known to be quoted as poetry.

TO MARY.

> The twentieth year is well-nigh past
> Since first our sky was overcast :—
> Ah, would that this might be the last !
> My Mary !

Thy spirits have a fainter flow,
I see thee daily weaker grow :—
'Twas my distress that brought thee low,
    My Mary !

Thy needles, once a shining store,
For my sake restless heretofore,
Now rust disused, and shine no more,
    My Mary !

For though thou gladly wouldst fulfil
The same kind office for me still,
Thy sight now seconds not thy will,
    My Mary !

But well thou play'dst the housewife's part,
And all thy threads with magic art,
Have wound themselves about this heart,
    My Mary !

Thy indistinct expressions seem
Like language utter'd in a dream :
Yet me they charm, whate'er the theme,
    My Mary !

Thy silver locks, once auburn bright,
Are still more lovely in my sight
Than golden beams of orient light,
    My Mary !

For could I view nor them nor thee,
What sight worth seeing could I see ?
The sun would rise in vain for me,
    My Mary !

Partakers of thy sad decline,
Thy hands their little force resign ;
Yet gently press'd, press gently mine,
    My Mary !

Such feebleness of limbs thou provest,
That now at every step thou movest,
Upheld by two ; yet still thou lovest,
    My Mary !

And still to love, though press'd with ill,
In wintry age to feel no chill,
With me is to be lovely still,
    My Mary !

But ah ! by constant heed I know,
How oft the sadness that I show
Transforms thy smiles to looks of woe,
    My Mary !

> And should my future lot be cast
> With much resemblance of the past,
> Thy worn-out heart will break at last,
>   My Mary!

Even love, at least the power of manifesting love, began to betray its mortality. She who had been so devoted, became, as her
mind failed, exacting, and instead of supporting her partner, drew
him down. He sank again into the depth of hypochondria. As
usual, his malady took the form of religious horrors, and he fancied
that he was ordained to undergo severe penance for his sins. Six
days he sat motionless and silent, almost refusing to take food.
His physician suggested, as the only chance of arousing him, that
Mrs. Unwin should be induced, if possible, to invite him to go out
with her; with difficulty she was made to understand what they
wanted her to do; at last she said that it was a fine morning, and she
should like a walk. Her partner at once rose and placed her arm
in his. Almost unconsciously, she had rescued him from the evil
spirit for the last time. The pair were in doleful plight. When
their minds failed they had fallen in a miserable manner under the
influence of a man named Teedon, a schoolmaster crazed with self-
conceit, at whom Cowper in his saner mood had laughed, but
whom he now treated as a spiritual oracle, and a sort of medium of
communication with the spirit-world, writing down the nonsense
which the charlatan talked. Mrs. Unwin, being no longer in a
condition to control the expenditure, the housekeeping, of course,
went wrong; and at the same time her partner lost the protection
of the love-inspired tact by which she had always contrived to
shield his weakness and to secure for him, in spite of his eccentric-
ities, respectful treatment from his neighbours. Lady Hesketh's
health had failed, and she had been obliged to go to Bath. Hayley
now proved himself no mere lion-hunter, but a true friend. In
conjunction with Cowper's relatives, he managed the removal of
the pair from Weston to Mundsley, on the coast of Norfolk, where
Cowper seemed to be soothed by the sound of the sea; then to
Dunham Lodge, near Swaffham; and finally (in 1796) to East
Dereham, where, two months after their arrival, Mrs. Unwin died.
Her partner was barely conscious of his loss. On the morning of
her death he asked the servant "whether there was life above
stairs?" On being taken to see the corpse, he gazed at it for a
moment, uttered one passionate cry of grief, and never spoke of
Mrs. Unwin more. He had the misfortune to survive her three
years and a half, during which relatives and friends were kind, and
Miss Perowne partly filled the place of Mrs. Unwin. Now and
then there was a gleam of reason and faint revival of literary faculty;
but composition was confined to Latin verse or translation, with one
memorable and almost awful exception. The last original poem
written by Cowper was *The Castaway*, founded on an incident in
Anson's Voyage.

" Obscurest night involved the sky,
    The Atlantic billows roared,
When such a destined wretch as I,
    Wash'd headlong from on board,
Of friends, of hope, of all bereft,
His floating home forever left

" No braver chief could Albion boast
    Than he with whom he went,
Nor ever ship left Albion's coast
    With warmer wishes sent.
He loved them both, but both in vain ;
Nor him beheld, nor her again.

" Not long beneath the whelming brine,
    Expert to swim, he lay ;
Nor soon he felt his strength decline,
    Or courage die away ;
But waged with death a lasting strife,
Supported by despair of life.

" He shouted ; nor his friends had fail'd
    To check the vessel's course,
But so the furious blast prevail'
    That pitiless perforce
They left their outcast mate behi
And scudded still before the wind.

" Some succour yet they could afford ;
    And, such as storms allow,
The cask, the coop, the floated cord,
    Delay'd not to bestow :
But he, they knew, nor ship nor shore,
Whate'er they gave, should visit more.

" Nor, cruel as it seem'd, could he
    Their haste himself condemn,
Aware that flight in such a sea
    Alone could rescue them ;
Yet bitter felt it still to die
Deserted, and his friends so nigh.

" He long survives, who lives an hour
    In ocean, self-upheld ;
And so long he, with unspent power
    His destiny repelled :
And ever, as the minutes flew,
Entreated help, or cried—' Adieu !' "

" At length, his transient respite past,
    His comrades, who before
Had heard his voice in every blast,
    Could catch the sound no more :
For then, by toil subdued, he drank
The stifling wave, and then he sank.

" No poet wept him ; but the page
  Of narrative sincere,
That tells his name, his worth, his age,
  Is wet with Anson's tear :
And tears by bards or heroes shed
Alike immortalise the dead.

" I therefore purpose not, or dream,
  Descanting on his fate,
To give the melancholy theme
  A more enduring date :
But misery still delights to trace
Its semblance in another's case.

" No voice divine the storm allay'd,
  No light propitious shone,
When, snatch'd from all effectual aid,
  We perish'd, each alone :
But I beneath a rougher sea,
And whelm'd in deeper gulfs than he."

The despair which finds vent in verse is hardly despair.   Poetry can never be the direct expression of emotion ; it must be the product of reflection combined with an exercise of the faculty of composition which in itself is pleasant.   Still, *The Castaway* ought to be an antidote to religious depression, since it is the work of a man of whom it would be absurdity to think as really estranged from the spirit of good, who had himself done good to the utmost of his powers.

Cowper died very peacefully on the morning of April 25, 1800, and was buried in Dereham Church, where there is a monument to him with an inscription by Hayley, which, if it is not good poetry, is a tribute of sincere affection.

Any one whose lot it is to write upon the life and works of Cowper must feel that there is an immense difference between the interest which attaches to him, and that which attaches to any one among the far greater poets of the succeeding age.   Still there is something about him so attractive, his voice has such a silver tone, he retains, even in his ashes, such a faculty of winning friends, that his biographer and critic may be easily beguiled into giving him too high a place.   He belongs to a particular religious movement, with the vitality of which the interest of a great part of his works has departed or is departing.   Still more emphatically and in a still more important sense does he belong to Christianity.   In no natural struggle for existence would he have been the survivor ; by no natural process of selection would he ever have been picked out as a vessel of honour.   If the shield which for eighteen centuries Christ, by His teaching and His death, has spread over the weak things of this world, should fail, and might should again become the title to existence and the measure of worth, Cowper will be cast aside as a specimen of despicable infirmity, and all who have said anything in his praise will be treated with the same scorn.